Jaybird in a Lei

Estee Kessler

CHAPTER ONE

A gruesome twosome comprising one knee skewering the vital spot of my gut and an accompanying elbow on my neck rousted me out of my comfortable slouch. I'd stocked my rented cabana with several sixes of quality beer to concentrate on my bellybutton mantra. The attacker behind both weapons destroyed any hope I might have had of spending a relaxed day on the beach. With the breath knocked out of me, I had all I could do to sit up.

Figures. Just one more disaster in a string of lousy encounters. Talk about a sucky twenty-four. Today was only one day in a succession of crass crappy days. Until this minute, I didn't think my day could get worse.

Last weekend, Marnie, my on-again-off-again girlfriend told me to go play with myself. "Consider us over," she'd said. "If I never set eyes on you again, that'd be too soon. I'm done wasting my time with an idiot who takes off and disappears with no notice and no apology anytime he feels like it. Makes for a good relationship—NOT. Find yourself another girl dumb enough, one not smart enough to consider the fact a guy's best friend is a bird as a clue for a total turn-off."

To make sure I didn't miss her point, she slammed the door when she left. Shut the thing so hard, she scared the stuff out of Peaches. Most days, Peaches, mom's cat is no scaredy- cat, but when Marnie did her nasty deed, she was with me to take a hit this time because I was cat sitting.

All of which meant my social life with both human and supernatural types sucked big time. What just happened to my groin made it worse.

Ditching me wasn't Marnie's fault—exactly—I understand lots of girls and some guys wouldn't want to spend time with a weirdo. I'm not, but I might appear weird to outsiders because J&R, the detective agency my partner Jakup and I run, handles some strange and outlandish cases. We take on clients with bizarre problems few experience and which other detectives won't touch.

Before I teamed up with Jakup, I wouldn't've wanted to spend time with a looney-tunes wacko like me either. Not that I'd make the frankly freaky list. Normal dudes, like I used to be, stick with the A-crowd types. My Greek row cred vaporized when I went over to the dark side...well, more like grayish side, supernatural, but not evil per se.

My plan was to give myself a week in Paradise after we closed our last case. Figured I might as well sit back and at least enjoy the scenery considering this might shape up to be a full week of serious babe watching. I opted to play at being normal and pretended I was. I didn't need to and won't do it again, but I took the red-eye to the Big Island, which gave me almost seven full days before I needed to head back to the mainland. What the hey, I deserved a break. If my lousy luck continued, when I got back, I'd get stuck on another sucky case with an obnoxious fat dude as a client.

Not much, I could do about it now. Gritting my teeth didn't help either—Marnie and I were history. Time to shed the funk. "Buck up, Riley Rose," I told myself.

My plan was to sit back, do nothing, and enjoy my time in Paradise. Now I was wearing the Mai Tai, I'd had in my hand before she'd ruined what remained of the day. The pressure of her leg on my thigh proved the little bit sunblock I'd rubbed on my most vulnerable parts—hadn't done their job. Well, at least no one had screamed, "Shark!" Score one on the plus side. I was the only one in trouble.

Until a few seconds ago, I'd concentrated on my tan. The beach view earned my overall Superb rating. Blondes, a few redheads, brunettes—all sporting well-built bodies and representing every race. The best part of beach-leering was none of 'em wore more three or four ounces of cloth. The body language of most on the sand sent the same message "Look-don't-touch."

Scrunched back into the shade of the half-ass cabana I'd rented for more money than it'd take to buy a dozen of crappy wannabe pup tents. I got the picture. Hawaiian sun was H O T. I wiggled in the ass-sling they called a beach chair to pull my swim trunks back down. I hate it when I give myself a wedgie.

Just before the blow to my stomach, I'd half-heard of a loud whap-whap outside my little patch of shade. I'd tilted my head, listening and trying to identify the source of the noise. All I got for my trouble was a shower of hot sand. The only thing I spotted was a shadow on the side of the cabana. The real whack to my midsection that followed came close to sending the stuff right out of me. For a minute,

I thought maybe my partner, Jakup, was the guilty party responsible for the racket. Wouldn't be the first time his wings beating against the canvas ruined my leisure time. When no sharp talons biting into my shoulder followed, I eliminated him from my list of possible perpetrators. We'd been partners for a long time. The fact Jakup is a scrub jay with...uh...-special abilities, limits who'd look up our detective agency. I suspected he enjoyed never executing a landing without drawing blood. Claimed this was just the way scrub jays set down. For once, I had a nearly healed shoulder because he'd taken his week off back in California. Seemed weird not to have him around.

"Uffda," I grunted when the shape solidified into a sweaty female shape and tripped over my outstretched legs. Her full weight fell on top of me.

Not a bad fall. All in all, a good fall—tall, brunette, D-D-G—and smelling good besides. In full panic mode, the girl didn't seem to even notice me, but crawled over my belly, kneeing another vulnerable spot, she scooted in high gear toward the back of the cabana.

"What the hell?" I asked. "Since when did I turn into your personal beach blanket?"

"I'm so sorry, but you got to help me," she said panting. "I can't let him catch me. This guy … he'll…He'll…he'll kill me—or enslave me. You've got to let me hide here. This is the only cabana big enough for two."

"Get a grip. Guys don't kill and enslave women these days. Went out with knights and armor. Gender equity and all that stuff all the rage now. Most girls don't pounce on some stranger, stick a knee in his gut, and talk smack. Why don't you j calm down and tell me what's going on?"

"Maybe most guys don't do stuff like that these days, but my ex doesn't seem completely human anymore. I'm not even sure he's even alive since—you've got to help me, please. I'm desperate."

Crap. I've just landed in it again. What if she wasn't 100% certifiable? What kind of supernatural mess am I in now? No doubt a bad one, considering my partner is nowhere around.

"Not human? C'mon. What does he run on four legs- some kind of angry pit-bull? You're exaggerating, making up metaphors about your psycho boyfriend."

"For real,—he's not human anymore, at least I don't think so. He's only half Leshy, but he seems to've inherited all their bad traits."

"Never heard of —what'd you call him—Leshy? Just because he's some ethnic I've never heard of doesn't make him inhuman. Maybe he just drinks too much. Could be that's your problem."

"No, not booze. Leshies aren't an ethnic. They're…well, something else. They don't drink—drink alcohol—at least. Most of them still live in the old country-- Serbia, Croatia, somewhere in that part of the world,

"Hold on, way too much information," I started, but she went right on talking, blowing me off.

"When we first met and started dating, Lief seemed like every other guy, you know, like totally full of himself. After he graduated U of M, his mom and dad sprung for him to visit relatives "back home." When he got back, I didn't know him anymore. Mean, nasty—and, he's gotten worse. I don't know what his relatives did, but since he got back, he's been spouting über-man ideas, and joined a supremacy cult—not the racial kind—more like, supernatural, I guess. I decided I needed to get away from him. Now he's followed me and has threatened me with all kinds of nasty things. You have to help me."

I wasn't sure if I'd just stepped in it or if my luck had turned and I'd met a girl familiar with the supernatural world—or possibly one who was downright nutso. I hesitated for a nanosecond or so, and then nodded. "Okay, I'll think about it. For now, let's blow this popcorn stand."

Her nose curled and I was afraid I'd came close to using the nerdiest expression ever, but she hugged me anyway. "Thank you, oh, thank you."

She'd said the last "Thank you" out when a big stump of guy blocked the sun coming into my Cabana. This was one big dude. He put his paw on my shoulder "Get your slimy hands off my girl," he growled, literally.

Talk about your living dead. I'd never seen a person with such white skin without even a trace of a sunburn. Arms so hairy he seemed to have a pelt, the effect of which was intimidating. He took one-step toward us and pulled off the cabana roof over us with one swift pass of his thick arm. I wanted no part of him and didn't need further proof he'd be dangerous to my health.

Putting my arms around her, I snuggled her in close sniffing in her perfume. I whipped up a screen I'd invented—well, stole from one of my mom's witchy books—to become invisible. He stood there, head going from side to side, confused.

Take that a-hole. Rip up my cabana and cost me a deposit, will you?

More growling and sniffing from the guy made the girl shake in my arms. I may - have held her a tad too close, but what the hell. When opportunity knocks, a guy's gotta answer.

CHAPTER TWO

Lief, aka the Ex, stomped off, cursing and kicking sand on every other sun worshipper he passed by,-spitting big loogies at the rest. A couple guys who evidently thought they were hot shots popped up, fighting mad acting ready to take him on until they got a good look at the size of their sand-kicker. I wouldn't have challenged him either. Meanwhile, I still didn't know the name of the girl sitting on my lap, but I was mega-aware of her ex who stood too tall, hefted too much muscle, and looked pissed-off enough to take on a water buffalo. I overheard the closest contender say, "Not worth it."

I agreed. Discretion and valor and all that sorta crap. I let the hazy force field hide the two of us melt away, but I changed my mind a couple seconds later and left part of the curtain over us to shield us from the searing sun overhead. Made sense seeing as the solar cook stove heat was the reason I'd shelled out for the cabana to start with. Too bad I didn't think of the force field thing before I dished out the cash. Would have saved me a sh-t-load of money. Kept me cooler, too.

The thought of what'd make a smart, sharp-looking chick like this whatever-her-name-was end up with a cretin (thanks Psych 101 for the fancy term for idiot) like Lief.

"Hillary."

"What?"

"Hillary, that's my name. Wasn't that what you were wondering?"

"Well, yeah, but how'd you know?"

"I...uh...I guessed. Once in a while, I...pick up on things from body language and...other stuff. My dad always claimed I got a double dose of women's intuition."

"I wouldn't know much about that," I said.

But I could guess. Intuition was more like this guy's an a-hole, that kind of thing, and not for me wanting to know her name. I speculated she might be a bit psychic, maybe even a little telepathic. What are the odds? For me, a world-class psychic, to meet up with another person—of the feminine persuasion no less—who might possess similar abilities— so soon after Marnie dumped me. Coincidence, I think not. The love gods had my back. Thank you, Cupid!

"About 257,050, 017 to 1," she said.

Done deal. She gave herself away. A telepath. First human I'd met with even a taste of this talent. My reaction was like what Homo sapiens called a gut reaction—vibes for the herb crowd and second sight for intellectuals. I gave myself a mental high five. Things definitely looked up—Lief aside, of course.

"That high? Wow. When did you realize not everyone caught on to what others were thinking? I didn't have a clue until my partner Jakup set me straight."

"Around my third birthday, I guess."

"No kidding?"

I was impressed. Either she qualified as a damn lucky with a little bit of ability or she actually possessed talent.

"I don't always catch what people are thinking this well. You seem...well...you seem easy to read."

Probably because I'm wide-open, broadcasting in every possible frequency. I've gotta watch that. I get sloppy when I'm around an all-human crowd. One day the wrong person might pick up something they shouldn't. I never expected to need to shield with a human.

"Whatever."

Until now, she'd been exactly where I wanted her, tucked up nice and close. Chest to chest but she decided to pull away and glance around, checking to see if Lief had doubled back. "I've got to leave. He's probably headed to the apartment I rented south of Kona. He'll trash everything I own. I can't let that happen. I spent almost all the money I had to get away from him and move here. Found this cute place to stay, and I won't let him destroy everything. I can't afford to replace everything."

I got the clear picture in her mind of her tiny apartment made locating where she lived a snap. Not far. Not so a good neighborhood. Didn't see much to worry about, she has hardly any furniture. "I can get us there toot sweet."

"I'm only a little way from here. I'll be careful walking. You don't need to."

"Sure, Hillary, until you run into Lief all by your lonesome."

She stopped short and turned toward me with a worried face. I continued, "If you're up for a new experience, I'll have you in your living room in less than a minute.

Her face said, "Sure thing...NOT."

Living room hell, a studio, and the scene she flashed me showed only one room, an incredibly cluttered one. What's the line on those cop shows? Been tossed?

"How...? she started, but I'd already 'ported the two of us to her place in a run-down near the coffee shakes south of Kona. She sputtered and shook when I put us down, side by side, on the couch/bed/futon.

"You ain't the only one with talent, Hillary."

"You teleport? Or do you take passengers when you have an out-of-body experience?"

Damn. She was quick. She must read a ton of science fiction; most folks don't even know what the words are, far less what they mean.

"Why do you say that? Maybe you passed out on the way over."

"No chance, since I've not swallowed a drop for weeks. Who can afford the good stuff and I don't do rotgut. I've read about how teleporting works, but I've never met anyone who could...could..."

"Get real Hil, "she whispered softly. I barely heard her. "Stuff like that is just for Trekkies. Doesn't happen in the real world."

I took pity on her. She'd nailed it, but was trying to convince herself otherwise. "Told you I got talents. Lots of 'em. Since Jakup and I took on that first case for Consolidated Covens, Witches Local 723 in the Wine Country, I've been perfecting one classy trick after another. Just ask Jakup. He'll back me up."

"You're nuts. I mean delusional. Reading someone and making a good guess on what's going on in their head is one thing, stuff like teleporting is way out there."

The sound of footsteps outside her door and the metal slam of the cover on the slot through her door spun us both around to face the door. False alarm. Mailman delivering advertising circulars. Her shoulders slumped in relief. No Lief.

"Look, Hillary, you need to grab what you need and stuff everything into a big garbage bag. If this guy is as bad as you say, we're both about to get a major case of island fever."

"I...I can't just leave. My job—"

"Jobs are replaceable. You might not be."

Now I'd scared her. Dealing with frightened victims was not new for me, and their reactions ain't pretty. I opened my mouth to continue when the familiar gouge of scrub jay talons cut through the sunburn on the tender parts of skin where I didn't manage to reach. My partner arrived. How did he make it all the way from the mainland? He's a good flyer, but ...

"Can't trust you for even a couple hours, Rose. One girl dumps your sorry ass and you gotta go trolling for another? What kind of partner is that? Give me a break."

"He talks. That bird talks. Now I know I'm hallucinating."

"Bird? Oh, that's only my partner, Jakup. I told you about him."

"You didn't tell me he was a freakin' talking bird. What kind of guy teams up with a bird?"

"A damn lucky one," my partner snapped. "What kind of girl teams up with the world's biggest idiot, hmmm?"

CHAPTER THREE

I stepped in between the two of 'em to prevent Hillary from whacking the feathers off my partner and, at the same time, block Jakup from a power climb up to build up acceleration for a daredevil dive-bomb on her hair. I gave him the benefit of the doubt and assumed he'd stick to typical scrub jay tactics and not try some nasty supernatural ploy. Talk about a couple hotheads. More bad karma for yours truly.

I released a mindsent scream to Jakup to defuse the situation. I set a strong shield so Hillary wouldn't tune in—assuming she was, in fact, telepathic and not a remarkably good guesser. "*Back off, blue blusterer. You might be supernatural, but this chick's got talent. Telepathic at least, I think, maybe more. We use her help on some of our cases .She didn't totally freak out when I 'ported her over here. How many humans do you know who'd react without leaving a brown blotch on their underwear?*"

At the same time, I said aloud to Hillary, "He's not always this tactless. Let me talk with him."

"*Aw- right, aw-right. I get it. I'll make nice.*"

"I still don't get why you'd have a bird as a partner."

He strutted across the couch toward her, holding out one wing. "Sorry, Hillary. I'm a little touchy—some nasty stuff going on. If Riley thinks you're okay, I'll give you a pass."

She looked over at me. "You've got two girls' names? Riley and Rose? Why've you got a girl's name?"

"You're kidding, right?" I turned toward her. "Riley is a boy's name, and, anyway, Rose is my last name."

"My best-girlfriend-from-High-School's name was Riley."

"Knock it off, you two," my partner said. "Let's not get hung up on assigning gender to names. We've got more important things on the table. For one, ditching Lief the Terrible before he comes back and does more damage to this place. And two, we need to move it— I got us a case back on the mainland. A big-bucks possible client coming around three—mainland time—which is in about an hour with the time difference. Let's get a trotting."

"You coming with?" I asked Hillary. "Gets you away from Lief for now. Until we have a plan, we aren't ready to deal with him.

"Coming whe...?"

I didn't give her time to finish. I packaged the three of us, teleported through the in between, and set us back in our borrowed office on the mainland. With luck, I might have found a girl. Someone I might actually be able to enjoy time with without having to answer to constant bitching about being gone all the time or having to come up with some lousy explanation. I wasn't able to take a chance of losing her before I made my first move on her.

I didn't expect a totally ticked off passenger when we arrived. "What gives you the right to just pick me up and deposit me wherever-you-damn-well-please, Mr. Riley Whatever? That's the second time you tried to play hero and carry off the damsel in distress. Buddy, I'm no damsel. "

I stared at her. Wasn't this the same girl who fell into my cabana begging for help? So now, if she didn't qualify as a damsel in distress, who did?

Jakup spoke up. "You'd rather Riley drop you off at your apartment so you can stay on the Big Island and meet up with Lief again? Or, if you like, he could drop you off by the Hindu temple over on Kauai— or perhaps you would prefer the lobby at the Marriott on Hawaii? We aim to please."

Without even a peek at Jakup, I was sure, if scrub jays could smirk, I'd find a shit-eating grin on his face.

"You don't have to be so sarcastic. I don't think I'd be asking too much to know where I was going before Mr. Big-Shot here scooped me up, then dropped me off who-knows-where. "

She had a point, a teeny, tiny point on the where-thing. We might have been in London or Tokyo or some obscure spot like Mobile. Alabama.

"And if we'd told you where, would everything be hunky-dory? What would you have done if you didn't come with us? Hmmm?" Jakup continued.

She'd picked the wrong person...uh...avian to pick a fight with. My partner had a short fuse and a quick tongue. Time for me to step in. I didn't want to lose my best shot at a real girlfriend I might find in years. This is the second time Jakup has gone off on a new client. He was downright nasty with Randy the Troll on our kidnapping case. I got it he didn't like trolls, but Hillary was one DDG human-style woman, capital W.

"Jakup, slow down, I said, "Hillary, we want to help you wherever you might be — Hawaii or Northern California. We also have an obligation to meet with a new client. You can wait in the lobby or, if this makes you uncomfortable, there's a great new restaurant a few doors down with strawberry waffles to die for."

Silence followed. This was a good sign. Signs of possible rationality creeping in?

More silence from Jakup, but Hillary said, "Sorry for being touchy. Lief has me so on edge, I'm not thinking straight. I'm so p**off with him. He's doing his best to ruin everything for me—my new job, my apartment in the best place a girl from Minnesota could hope for. No snow, no sleet."

Her voice trailed off. I waited.

"All right, all right," Jakup said. "My wings are damn near falling off—I only caught updrafts once in a while. Haven't made a trip like that since I went along with a couple blackbird friends on their migration. Haven't done it since. I took on freelance work for the Consolidated Covens."

I stared at him. "You're kidding, right? You didn't fly to Kauai, did you? Like on your own wings? I wondered why you just showed up."

"Nah, couldn't help pulling your chain. I hitched a ride with United. A cushy spot in the first class galley. Well stocked, too. Avila at Witches local 723 scryed your location for me."

"You are one weird bird," I said.

Hillary's head tilted from side to side eying us. "Uh, how far is that restaurant you mentioned. I am so hungry. The last time I was early yesterday. I took off when I found out Lief showed up. How long do you think this client confab might last?"

I looked over at Jakup. He set this up. He did his how-the-hell-should-I know head cock. So what else is new?

"Why don't you give us an hour—if this guy is still here, you can wait in the lobby. I got one of those coffee things with the little plastic doohickeys my mom says are filling up the solid waste sites."

"Wow, I didn't take you for a tree hugger type, going all environmentalist," she said. "Right or left out the door?"

"Down two floors, left. Elevator is at the end of the hall."

"Okay. See you in sixty."

She headed out, and I sat down on the couch in the waiting room. "What've you got us into this time?"

"A referral from the two guys we met down in Solvang. "

"You mean Chuck and Bob? The two Werewolves who played for USC?

CHAPTER FOUR

When our visitor arrived, I gave my forehead a mental swat –the newcomer ranked way over déjà vu all over again. How come we only attract the strange? I'd much rather deal with a resident of the real world than any more supernatural characters. This one was a near miss as ugly as Randy, our last client. Ugly could act as a synonym for a troll. Randy was proof. On that case, we'd rescued her little sister Merilee, who, in fairness, turned out to be a smart kid who wanted to be a nurse. Saving her still made me feel good and made time spent with Randy seem less ghastly. Randy had lived up in every way to the tarnished troll reputation.

Yucky gross was one thing, but my eye-gut coordination was working overtime because right this minute I was more than a little queasy just looking at him...it. Eyes front and straight on, the room appeared empty, but, if I tipped my head to one side, a darkish shape appeared in my peripheral vision. The there-not-there-being gave me a distinct urp moment. Trying to focus in on something this way was like being behind the wheel in heavy traffic and trying to read a license plate on the car next to you while keeping your eyes on the road ahead so you to avoid causing a world-class a pile-up. The numbers get all fuzzy and the car whips past you forcing you to speed up.

Having to rely only on the corner of my eye made me dizzy. By the time, I spotted a ghostly image of a swarthy dude, slithery-shadowed, tall and skinny I was ready to pop my cookies. Jakup didn't seem to have the same problem as I did. Science types say birds can see what's not in front of 'em all the time. I kept my mouth shut. This'd be one more thing for Jakup to boast about.

"What can we do for you, Sir?" he asked what seemed to be to be a vacant space in front of us.

"Two of my friends from USC suggested I get in touch with you. They're special guys and I...happened to mention my problem to them."

"SC, you're kidding, right? I said.

"Nope. We were on the same football team although they graduated a semester before I did. Chuck and Bob played the line, right and left tackle. I was more of a special plays kind of guy. When the coach called for an unexpected end-round run, he tapped to carry the ball. The guys on the other team usually didn't...uh...spot me right off— plus I'd outrun them."

I couldn't help blurting out, "You played football at SC? If you don't mind me asking, considering how shadowy...I mean, the difficulty in...seeing—tell me, how?" I didn't ask how the referee would wave him in—or his teammates could pull off a play if they couldn't see him, but the thought did cross my mind.

"*He is smiling at you,*" Jakup mindsent me realizing I wasn't able to focus on much of the guy.

The mental picture I got of an orphan pigskin drifting downfield and bouncing off the end zone for a touchdown cleared up a lot for me. "So you're the reason we kept losing to the Trojans? Trust USC to throw in a ringer."

"On the contrary, my name appeared on the roster, and I was a legitimate full-time student. I majored in quantum biology. My specialty was the quantum superposition of wild vertebrates, concentrated on reptiles, but dealt with mammals as well. It's a new discipline."

"Say what?"

Jakup, as usual, interrupted, "Very interesting, Mr.?"

"You can call me Doug. My real name is impossible an average ...American... to pronounce.

Why the hesitation? What was he going to say? Probably some derogatory name for my species or some kind of put-down about humans. I'd put money on it. What did USC put in the program for him? And who are you calling average? Why are supernatural types always putting down humans? Like whatever-they-are is so special.

"I've had considerable success since I graduated. I've worked full time and attended grad school, got my masters. I'm planning to publish my first paper next spring. I...have an advantage over others in the same field. My subjects aren't able to see me until I've finished my observations which lets me observe them more for extended periods of time."

I put my mouth in gear, but Jakup blindsided me. "Doug, what you say leads me to conclude you've done okay on your own. I don't understand why you came to meet with us?"

Jakup was pulling his ever-so-professional act, but the voice from the blank space by the window didn't respond at first. He cleared his throat and began, "I met this girl a few months ago. She works in the same lab as I do. Her name is Darcy. Long story short, we've hit it off, and I'd like to move things up a notch, maybe get married someday."

I couldn't hold it in. "How does someone like you, one most humans can't see, get a date? Doesn't compute."

"My body is like yours except I'm not visible to everyone. For example, when I played football, the equipment covered most of me including my head. My teammates and folks in the stands saw a football uniform in a helmet run down the field. Most of the time they didn't notice my face wasn't showing. Off the field, I wore hoodies a lot, and I bought out the local theatre supply of face make-up. When I got to USC I applied some of the stuff I was learning to my own situation and...uh...devised a better way to make myself appear corporeal from whatever angle my companion observed me. Took me a while to learn what thickness I needed for the outer...uh...layer. Maybe the best way to describe my process would be to call the result a full body mask. All in all, the technique was a heck of a lot less messy."

"Okay, so what's your problem then?

"What I do to compensate takes a lot of concentration—all my energy to maintain the appearance of the parts not covered is a big deal. Darcy's been talking about going swimming this summer at her parent's cabin in the mountain and...other things--I won't be able to pull off a whole body cover. If I slip up, I lose the love of my life."

He sounded hysterical. Not very manly. I'll bet she's the only girl who's ever gave him the time of day. Love in the lab. I didn't want to imagine what she looked like. GREAT – all this is because he wants to get naked with a girl.

"Again, Doug," my partner said in a snooty way, "As you've apparently solved your problem already, why do you need J&H? We are a busy firm—we need to ration the time available for our many clients."

We do?

"Of, course; I realize you must carry a full caseload. Chuck and Bob spoke well about you--something about the work you did in Solvang? They didn't get into any detail, but I've known them for a long time and trust their judgment."

Both of us ignored his question. Client confidentiality and all. We're professionals, after all.

"Ancient history, Dude. What Jakup said." I said.

"Okay, the thing is my great-aunt Bltsvique told me years ago our family used to be corporeal. We were the next thing to human on the food chain and lived the good life on Easter Island. Most of us have moved on to other islands in the Pacific. Most folks recognize us from the statues of our ancestors they've seen in tourist photos. Some generations ago, a shirttail cousin traded our perceptibility for...for god-knows-what. He didn't share his loot with the rest of us. We never found out for sure the person he traded with. Most likely, the seller wasn't some peace or Wisdom Goddess. A good guess might point to another avatar for the war god—druid or Norse or possibly the Japanese Kami-no-Kaze."

"For many in the family, our semi-invisibility ended up as a great career opportunity. Took camouflage to a whole new level. I've got several uncles who were successful second-story men, for example. But for a guy like me, one who wants to move freely in the human world, date a girl, being the way I am ain't so great."

"Look, Buddy," I interrupted. "That's fine and all, but answer the question. Why us? We're not scientists or magicians. My mom's a kick-ass witch, but I know for a fact, she doesn't mess with stuff like this either."

"My mother used to tell me stories about a talisman, the Mark of Camael, a mystic tablet with the power to make us appear like other humans again. After I met Darcy, I remembered what she'd said and thought this might be a way to reverse my condition. Solid, I'm relatively sure I'd still qualify as human—my people all were way back when. You got to help me. I'm in love, got it bad. I need you to find the Mark for me."'"

Jakup and I looked at one another and had the same thought. Yes-sure-ree-Bob— thought you'd never ask. Find a tablet where? You got a clue the spot on the globe we might look? Like the thing we'd be trying to find would be made of what? How big? With our luck guarded by some nasty creature at least a couple hundred years old with big teeth. Not likely."

Jakup spoke up first...or at least he intended to. The outer door opened, and Hillary breezed in.

"Why're you guys talking to an empty room?"

CHAPTER FIVE

"What's this Kū-ka-ili-moku guy gotta do with any of this?" I asked, ignoring my partner who'd turned his head and clacked his beak. A sure sign he thought I should shut my trap, as my dad used to say.

Kū-ka-ili-moku is the Hawaiian avatar of Kukulkan, the war god. The Mark belonged to Mars, the ancient god of war in Europe. If you think about what's happened in history, the war gods've booked a good run. War has always been with us, omnipresent, I guess you'd say."

Ye gods, yawn city. No, I wouldn't say omnipresent or omni-anything for that matter. The last thing I want to listen to is some dumb lecture about some has-been gods.

"On the Kona coast where I grew up, Kū-ka-ili-moku was a big-shot, a kahuna, a heavy hitter. A local tourist attraction was a few blocks from our house with this temple thing and a mongo statue of him standing in the middle. The thing used the scare the crap out of me standing there with his mouth hanging open."

'*This guy is a nut job,*" I mindsent Jakup. "*Let's get rid of him and deal with Hillary's case.*"

"*The nut job can afford our fee. We're not walking out of that just because you've got the hots for some chick.*"

"*Even society attorneys take a pro bono case on occasion.*"

"*Yeah? Name one.*"

When I couldn't, Jakup flew up and perched on the chair nearest Doug's floating head. "Doug, you've got to help us here. Riley made a special trip back to meet with you. We need more than old family stories if we're going to help you. We need to know what to look for, when and where the tablet—Mark or whatever you call the thing—was last seen, and, more importantly, why you think this would be useful for you. Going in circles doesn't accomplish much. "

At this, the air chilled, like 20 or 30 degrees. Maybe Doug wasn't as human as he professed to be...or as sincere. Was his story of being human and in love a tale to entice us into a dangerous situation?

Hillary noticed the change, too. "Don't you guys heat this place? My teeth are chattering. I've lived on Hawaii long enough to get used to warm weather."

"Oh, sorry, "Doug said, "I didn't mean to do that. If our emotions get out of kilter, they nudge the temperature up or down, one of the side effects of my family's condition. Generally, I've better control, needed to, what with living and working with normals as I do. Until I met Darcy, I'd never experienced such vibrant positive emotion. I'm in a bind; she wants to spend a week at the cabin at the end of the month—that means the naked thing. She'll expect me in a swimsuit...or less. I would need to go whole all the time all over. I've looked for a solution on my own, talked with my mom, my aunt Beti, and even my grandfather who's got dementia for some clues. Nada. J&H is my last hope for love."

"Why?" I demanded. "If you're as smart as you say you are, why don't you just take care of business?"

"You need hear the whole story. I'm not the first to try becoming visible to assimilate. We're not all criminals or passive bystanders. Many of us admire some things humankind accomplishes, but freak with sheer terror at what they're doing to muck up the planet we both call home. I'm not the first in my community to fall in love with a normal. The legend among my people is that the Romeo and Juliette story was about two of us, not some underage Italians with mixed up hormones and a family problem. The ancestor who sold us out for the tablet didn't just mess with us. He pissed off the war gods. They don't like folks bartering off their possessions to humans. Whenever humans get involved in god business, they always foul up the works. These gods don't want their plan for the world gummed up They think if anyone is to retrieve Camael's Mark , one of 'em should—and, if they do, all hell breaks loose for the rest of us. Adding the power of the Mark on top of the nefarious natural skills of their fraternity, they'd be free to create havoc, incite nation against nation, mother against daughter, father against son. No pet dog will be safe. Bottom line, if one or a group of allied war gods reaches the tablet first, we've all got a big problem. Worse than open-pit mining and air pollution ever thought about being. A rumor is floating around they located a clue which is getting 'em close. My concerns are personal. I love Darcy, but you've all got a stake in this, too."

I brought up the image Buster, the overweight lab who lived with my mom and dad back home. Nobody messes with my dog. God or no god.

"We'll take your case," I said

CHAPTER SIX

Hillary gave me a variation of the look my mom used to use on me when I was a little kid. Whoa, what did we do to deserve that?

"I'm beginning to think I've walked into the set of Grimm—monsters coming out of the wall, supernatural conspiracies. Is this what you deal with all the time?"

Maybe she had a point. I'd never considered my life to be an episode in a TV series. Maybe it should be—at least then they'd pay me a potful for my troubles. There were days I wished I'd listened in my Psych 101 class. Everybody who came to J&H had a problem they wanted to lay on me. Every Were and Shape-shifter thought they needed a shrink. I guess there weren't many supernaturals working the psychoanalysis game. . Of course, the fact I was an expert inter-species communicator might have something to do with it. On the other hand, how does Hillary get off being so high and mighty - wasn't she the one mixed up with a violent Leshy?

She must have caught my thought because she continued, "I admit I may have dipped a toe into the supernatural world when I started dating Lief, but until he went to visit relatives in Serbia, he seemed like any of the others guys I'd dated. He was great. Lots of fun, maybe a bit too much of a practical joker, but otherwise, a perfect boyfriend."

"Now you realize he's not. What do you expect us to do?" We've agreed to take Doug's case. His problem is more in line with others we've pursued," Jakup said in that snarky too-professional-tone he uses when he's trying to get out of something or impress the hell out of someone who could care less.

"I don't think I ever did ask you to take my "case," as you call it. I needed to get away from Lief, and Riley's cabana was a convenient place to hide. Next thing I know, I'm here, somewhere I never asked to be, thanks to you," she said, pausing. "Still, hiring you might be the thing I need to do. Maybe the way he's been acting has something to do with him being part Leshy. Maybe Leshy isn't just an obscure ethnic group in Serbia like I'd thought."

"You're sayin' he might be the sort of villain we'd be interested in?" I asked.

She didn't answer. She stared at me with blank, unfocused eyes and, after a short pause, she shook her head. "Maybe."

I glanced over at the disembodied hand and arm and the shell of a face and said, "Doug, she had a point. We can't discriminate one supernatural over another."

"You ever heard of a Leshy?" I mindsent Jakup.

"I think they're some kind of elf-pixie-sprite shape-shifter. If we agree to take her case, I'll check in with Betty at OWIS."

"If? Uh huh. We're doin' it. No way I'm going to blow the best chance I've had in a long time for a girlfriend."

"Your love life is supposed to be the decider?"

"And yours isn't?

Neither of 'em heard us, but they sensed something was going on with us. And it was. We were getting real close to moving on to physical confrontation and starting to circle one another when Doug's voice broke in.

"Look, Guys, if you're trying to decide which one of us to work with first, why not join forces. Seeing as both of us need to deal with a problem on the Big Island, why not join forces? Strength in numbers, so to speak. I help Hillary out of her rude man-unlove story—she helps me get in mine. From my corner, having a girl on board might be a good thing. Give us some insight into how my girl might react if...if she finds out what I really am."

"I'm game, "I said giving Hillary a smarmy smile.

"Lemme get this straight. We'd be taking two cases, but working both together. One client helps the other and vice versa. Both owe a fee, right?"

Hillary grimaced at the word fee, but nodded nevertheless. 'I'm in."

No problem. She could pay her fee in kind.

Doug's face moved up and down rapidly. The flat slice of face brought on the urp factor again. "I'm in, too," he said.

My heart gave a little thump, skip, and jump. I'd won the daily double – double fees and spending more time with the most remarkable and best-built girl I'd met yet.

Hillary's mouth twisted to one side in disgust. She must have caught my remark about her... endowments. I wasn't prepared for another person overhearing me—or whatever they call eavesdropping into another's thoughts.

I was admiring Hillary's silhouette outlined in the glass-block wall when the wave of cold nausea struck me.

CHAPTER SEVEN

"What's wrong, Riley? Hillary asked in a concerned tone. "You got this strange look on your face—you act as if you spotted one of your monsters coming at you out of nowhere. I've never seen anyone freeze in place like you did, or stand so still so long since—well, ever."

I heard Jakup chuckle. "Best statue act I've had since my stay at Trafalgar Square."

I hurt too much to be pissed. The mother-of all-cramps seized my whole body. Every cell locked in place. Think of the time you came up lame with a hamstring or the pain inflicted when your big toe heads in a direction it shouldn't. Now multiply by, say, a couple thousand and you might come close to the hurt I had. The shock of my pre-cog moment stiffened me and left me rigid. Putting my thoughts into words took a while, and I needed to put every effort into sputtering out what I wanted to say.

"What the hell are we thinking, Partner, going against a combined army of every war god since the beginning?" I blurted out. "They know we're coming for the Mark thing. I don't know how or why they know or why they think we are such a big deal, but they do. Them being gods and spread out around the globe might explain it."

Jakup didn't say a word, but Doug asked. "How do you know?

"Didn't your buddies Chuck and Bob, the football players from SC tell you Riley was a world-class pre-cog?"

"Uh, no,"

"What's a pro-cog?" from Hillary.

"Not pro-cog, pre-cog. A pre-cog is someone who cheats the casinos," Jakup said. "Hey, that's a cheap shot. Wasn't like I did it deliberately," I countered.

"He claims," Jakup said in an ultra-sarcastic tone, "he didn't realize he could tell which slot machine would pay off, which number would come up on the roulette wheel. He tried to convince me he was "just lucky."'

"Well, maybe not *lucky* lucky, but I never intended to cheat."

'That's the worst part," Jakup said, turning toward Hillary. "He'd been gaming the casinos for years without a clue. Didn't have the sense to realize the reason for his "luck" was reading the future, not some dealer's tell."

"Do what? Read what future?" the two-person chorus asked.

"Yeah, he's exaggerating like he always does. I've got my limitations. I can't predict world events for crap and most things I sense happen in the next day or so, a week tops. Even then, at times, but not all times. If Jakup and I, or even just me, are involved I get flickers, skimpy glimpses of what's coming down, especially one which might create a big wave—I do better with reading images of past events. I do that all the time."

Hillary and the plate-faced quantum biologist exchanged a knowing glance. His head wobbled, and she shook hers. I didn't need to be a psychic to read they were thinking. "Bullshit!"

"You are both nuts. I'm better than average on the fringe stuff, guessing someone's name or occupation, but everyone knows the future's not ours to tell," she lip-synched.

"Maybe not for most humans, but my partner has surprised the supernatural world with his abilities. We must assume he is right and begin our plans for how we accomplish Doug's goal, talk some sense into Lief, and stay alive."

Holy shit, Batman. Was this my partner? The scrub jay with the world's most sarcastic tongue? This is the second time Jakup has talked me up. Would wonders never cease?

"Wha—did you say to stay alive?"

My partner calmly walked across the table and up my leg and, nose to beak said, "'Riley, think about what you just said. They know. A pack of pissed off war gods knows we're after one of their prized possessions. Did you think when we found it, they'd say, 'Why, of course, dear Riley, we'd be happy to let a puny human like yourself take the Mark of Camael away from us'"

Describing the gods' reaction in this way seemed a bit on the optimistic side. "Then what do you suggest, great all-knowing multi-feathered detective?"

"Doesn't take rocket science to figure this out, Hotshot. The war gods had it made for a good century or two, millennia probably, and they want back the perks and the power they once commanded. They were big shots for a long time—with no contenders. They'd cherry pick the mortals to carry out what they wanted. Mars instigated a potful of battles all around the Mediterranean. His cousins Camolos and Tyr teamed up to keep the fires of the Napoleonic Wars going. Sometimes a war god possessed a mortal to accomplish his or her aims – think Alexander the Great. They concentrated on their own backyards. The brouhaha they stirred up in Germany was there latest and best effort. They scored big time with their man Adolf, but they overlooked one thing, made the conflict too long, too widespread, and too sadistic. Too many humans worldwide got involved. They picked up a few things. In fact, they turned out to be fast learners. Humans were making these gods obsolete. Men could handle murder and mayhem on that scale almost on their own. Humans finally succeeded at something—unfortunately."

"Like scrub jays are so perfect." I had to say.

He ignored me. Scrub jay cheek in full force now. "Unless Riley is once again mistaken—and we can't rule that out—now the gods want their old game back on. They want to call the plays, put their own guys in as captains."

The silence hurt. What could two humans, a bird, and what-ever-in-hell-Doug-was do against an army of bloodshed professionals intent on war?

"I don't like the odds, but what choice do we have? We've already kicked the shit-pile when we agreed to take Doug's case. And, even if we hadn't, preventing a worldwide bloodbath is the right thing to do." Jakup said.

Who could argue with logic like that?

"Let's get to it"

"I'm in."

"Me, too"

"You'll need a leader," said Jakup. "Fortunately..."

"You've got one," I said.

CHAPTER EIGHT

Jakup rolled on the floor, laughing hysterically. "You? ...Leader?...Right leader...you?...Great one, Partner. Funniest thing I've heard in a long time. Hee Hee Hee...oh, boy!" He was kicking his feet in the air, talons glistening in the light from the window. Feathers flew.

"Like some kind of blue-feathered dervish might be," I groused. Enough is enough. I sneaked a glance over at our dumbfounded clients for their reaction.

"And it's not like your spinning top act is one to instill confidence in us from Doug and Hillary—who are, after all, our clients. Or did you forget?" I mindsent.

He did his best imitation of the baleful raven stare, pretzeled his body upright, and started toward me.

"Come on you guys, grow up. Do I have to be the mom here?" Hillary asked.

At the magic word mom, I straightened up. Jakup turned toward her, and said, "He's my leader and you're my mom. I don't think so."

'When you two finish acting like kids from some pre-school, we have research and planning to do. Good thing there is a woman here to keep us all on track. Our goals," she said, "are to get Lief gone for me, and Darcy to end up with Doug
. Do you two, by any remote chance, have anything in mind. Likes ideas we could use to accomplish our objective?"

Doug's visible body parts moved up and down. "She's right, you know. We've got some work to do before we set up camp on Mauna Kea."

I hated to admit it—after all, we guys had her outnumbered three to one, p

'Sorry, Partner," Jakup sent me.

"Me, too."

The air cleared and my mouth opened to share my wisdom when Doug and Hillary started to talk at the same time. Like in a chorus, they said, "We need to know who our opponents are. Where they might be weak and what their strengths are..."

"I'll check at OWIS for the work-up on the Mark, on Leshies overall and maybe something on the Hawaiian god scene—who's in and who's out, that kind of thing," Jakup offered.

"OWIS?" The chorus chimed.

"Other World Information Service. Kind of like Deeperweb or one of the NSA's snoop search programs but with tons more on the supernatural stuff human databases don't have."

"Check with Betty to see if there are gods on the big island on our side that we might bunk with while we look for the Mark," I suggested. "Maybe discover who the rest of the players might be."

"Why not just stay in a hotel? Or at my apartment? Hillary asked.

The image of the cluttered mess of her place flashed an image in my head. I didn't want to dis the place but OMG. It'd be like moving into a dumpster, sans rodents. "Um, that's a possible, but..."

"Something safer and more defensible would be better if things get hot,' Jakup said. My relatives are smart enough to head for the high wires when a cat or snake invades their nesting area. They'd put distance between 'em and the nasties out for a good meal."

"From what Riley told me, your place wouldn't be big enough for the four of us," Doug said.

"We could split up into teams, might be more efficient. You and Jakup look for the Mark thing and Hillary and I will take on her ex," I said in a hopeful tone. *Talk about advantages—what could be better than an intense joint venture with a beautiful babe I could really get into?*"

"*Nice try, Partner*," Jakup sent. "*Not a chance.*" Aloud he added, "There's strength in numbers."

Unfortunately, Hillary jumped on his bandwagon. "I agree, splitting up would be a mistake for us. I vote for our original plan. The team approach makes more sense. Each of us has some unique talents. "

Any vision I'd had of some quick cannoodling overlooking the sea vaporized. *I never catch a break. What's wrong with earning a buck or two while putting the make on a girl you like?*

Jakup paced back and forth on the table, his claws clicking. "You humans will need a place to sleep, three beds, right?"

"Uh...I started. " If we had to, we might get by with two."

"You're going to sleep with Doug?" Hillary asked. "Are you sure Doug's down with that?"

Doug and I stared at each other aghast. "Spoon with another guy? I don't think so," splatted across both our faces. "No, "we chorused.

Hillary stood u0, staring at me, breathed deep, and shook her head in a way that left me zero room for argument. No indoor canoodling either, I guess.

"I've got a suggestion," Doug said. "At work, we always try to design our workspace large enough to work efficiently, but not so big that the space becomes cumbersome. We analyze before we start what equipment we'll need and try to have everything on hand. Once we're equipped and settled, work begins. Of course, if I'm out in the field, and my subjects might be considered dangerous, I add in provisions for safety and ample food."

"Food's good," I said. "Anyone else hungry."

Icy looks my way.

"Okay. Three beds. Room for equipment, food, and enough isolation to not attract attention. That about sum up what we need?" My partner said.

"We can't all sleep in the same room," Doug said. "Darcy'd have my head if she found out, assuming I get everything worked out, and she'll still have me."

I pursed my lips and remembered one brochure I read when I decided I needed some time in paradise. "I know just the place. The Presidential Suite at the Fairmont. You remember it was the Orchid? Ocean view, cool master bedroom, a couple lanais, and, the suite comes with access to the Gold Floor so we'd eat breakfast free."

The reaction from all but Hillary was a blank stare. Hillary, on the other hand, said in a frosty tone, "And the cost for all that?"

"Not so bad—the fifth night is free, if we're there that long," I argued.

"Not a problem," said Doug. "I inherited a trust fund I could tap if I can't hack their computer to give us a good discount...or free."

I'm liking this dude more and more. I wonder what other surprises he has for us. I'm glad he's stuck on Darcy, because, otherwise, Hillary might get some bad ideas.

"Everybody game for the Fairmont?" I asked.

Heads bobbed.

Prestige and pampering coming up.

CHAPTER NINE

While Doug worked his magic on our reservation, I lobbied for lunch. Convincing the other was more difficult than I'd expected because I was the only one hungry. I was kinda used to this, but this time I wasn't the only male in the group.

"We can get a takeout cold plate when we get there. Teriyaki something and rice." Hillary said.

"C'mon, guys, I've got at least one heavy load to take over, maybe two. I need fuel. "

We argued but not much longer before they agreed. I'd call what the group exhibited less than stellar enthusiasm, but I'd prevailed. No big whoop. I picked up lunches at the pita joint down the street. I polished off my lamb and cucumber pita and half of Doug and Hillary's. Jakup pecked at his food like always. Now I was ready to 'port.

"Okay, you got everything you need? Laptop? Deodorant? Toothbrush? Clean underwear? You're sure you won't need anything more because I ain't making repeat trips. Too damn cold. Which reminds me, you've got sweaters?"

Doug didn't and seemed confused at why he'd need one, but I loaned him the ratty green one anyway. "Aw right, looks like we're ready to go. I'll take Doug and Jakup first. I don't think I can handle three human types at once. Doug, you can stay solid long enough for the hop, right?"

I could tell from how he was standing, my partner knew I was lying about the load and just wanted to get Hillary close again. Doug looked around, "Hop? Why should I hop? Can't I..."

Before he had the words out of his mouth, I'd whiffed both of 'em to our destination. Damn, I'm good. Didn't lose either one of 'em.

"Hey, not half bad," I said looking around. "I could get used to this." I let go of Doug and headed for the sandbox. 'Porting did that to me.

When I got back to the main room, what I could see of Doug was staring out the window. "I wish Darcy could be here to see this," he said.

"Buck up, Dude, that's what we're here for. Why don't you get settled, and I'll pick up the rest last of our valiant band of crime fighters."

He seemed okay with my plan, so I grabbed a soda out of the mini-bar and headed back for Hillary and the best part of the trip.

When I appeared next to her on the couch, she started and her eyes got wide. "You're back already? Like... no time at all. I didn't think teleporting was an in and out kind of thing. Seemed to take forever getting here."

"I read somewhere the normal time-space continuum doesn't work right with 'porting. Times seem longer there than here. You ready to go?"

She nodded, and, wonder of wonders, put her arms around me and settled in my lap. Heaven is right here, right now. Hoo boy. I pulled her in tight enough to sniff her perfume. "Don't want to drop you," I explained. I wished I knew a way to slow the trip down.

"Took you long enough," Jakup said.

"What are you talking about? He was hardly gone at all, Doug protested. "Chuck and Bob never told me you could teleport. They just said you understood interspecies communication and did a bang-up job on the Wereweasel case."

"We'll put it on the list," my partner said. "Doug, what else haven't you mentioned besides the trust fund, anything useful?"

"And how did a lab rat like you get a trust fund anyway," I added. "Most researchers are lucky to eat, and I thought you said your family were sea-faring islanders, not wealthy big-shots."

"Remember I told you about my uncles who ...made it big in the B&E trade? I guess they felt a little guilty about what they did. They set some small trust funds up for their nieces and nephews. I've never touched any up until now. I don't like living off of illegal activities."

"Hacking is legal?" I asked.

"Most of the time," he answered. "Well, besides the transparent thing, my work in quantum makes me look at things in an all-inclusive all distant way. I can out-analyze the best of them."

Oh, goody. Aren't you special?

Hillary's pen was moving. She was making a list. "I don't have much to add. I've got a gift for intuition, and I read most people better than average."

But you've got other attributes, I thought, staring at her chest. "Jakup flies and has twenty-four-seven access to a cool search engine. I'm a pre-cog, psychic, teleport, and am an all-around wonderful guy. That should sum up what we're putting in the game."

A long silence followed. "Sounds like we've put down everything we have to list," said Hillary. "Now the question is, what advantages do our opponents have?"

"Or who are our opponents?" Doug added. "How many? How close? For that matter, does the Mark have some kind of built-in protection against others?"

"Not a great backfield for the game," I said—to blank looks. No other football players in the crowd apparently.

"Thank you for that valuable observation," Jakup said in an artificial saccharine tone. "Is anyone interested in what I've found out so far from OWIS?"

Then Hillary's cell chirped.

"Lief, I told you not to call me? And you've got some stones to even try after what you did to my apartment."

She stopped and her face went pale. "How..."

She looked down, staring at her phone. "He knows where I am."

CHAPTER TEN

Hillary went weird white. She was looking down at her phone, a lost expression on her face. "He says he knows where I am and trying to run away again won't work. Oh, and he said, 'That interfering bastard who took me from him better watch his back.'"

Me? An interfering bastard?

"Hillary, calm down," Doug said. "All he knows is what transmission tower your signal is coming from, not where you are. His best shot would be a forty mile circle to search, and maybe farther. Just to be safe, though, let me check your phone. I did my share of phone hacking back in my college days when I was too poor to pay for a decent plan."

Hillary moved like a zombie and handed Doug her cell. I had to wonder what other special skills he'd failed to mention.

Doug cracked the phone and poked around the guts. I didn't think cells phones came apart. He pulled some strange multi-blade tool from an invisible pocket and walked over to the window where he slanted the cell toward the light to check the board inside. He poked at the contents before slapping the parts back in place and handing Hillary back her phone. "The good news is I don't see anything suspicious right off, but did this poor excuse for a boyfriend ever have your phone—like for more than a few minutes?"

"Now I think of it, yes. Once. Over a weekend when things were going good between us."

"In that case, take the batteries out of this thing and buy a new phone. Your best option would be a pre-paid. What the street folks call a burner phone. Does anyone need to know your new number?"

She hesitated. "Besides my mother, no."

"Why? I asked, just to keep myself in the conversation.

"Because the fewer people who know the number, the better," Jakup said in that know-it-all tone of voice I hated so much. "The only one here who'd need a phone would be Doug. You and I can communicate without a device."

"You're telling me that bastard may have bugged my phone?" she asked Doug.

"Either with a super-tiny bug or a virus," Doug answered nodding.

"That bastard. That freakin' bastard," she growled.

"Why would he do this? Bugging his girlfriend's phone seems a little over the top. I mean talk about jealous," I said.

"Super possessive he was. At first, I kind of liked how close he clung to me, but as time went on, I began to see his behavior as controlling."

"I agree tampering with your phone seems excessive if we're talking about a jealous lover," Jakup said. "Didn't you say when he returned from a visit overseas he'd changed?"

"Yes, he turned nasty—so much so I dumped him."

"You mentioned groups he'd taken up with in Europe. His personality change is too coincidental. Quite likely whoever-they-are- put him up to it for reasons of their own—wherever or whatever they are,"

"We are so AFU! Now Lief has a posse, too. Isn't it enough we have to deal with a bunch of conniving war gods, now we've got another slimy batch of scuzzballs against us?" I asked.

"Pretty much," Doug answered. "But what the hell is SOAFS?"

"Shit on a fu..."

"I get it," he said nose curling. He turned toward Hillary, "Okay. Keep the batteries out until you have the replacement. Call your mother and give her the number—ask her not to tell anyone else. Hint at Lief being..."

"Difficult," she said. "That's how I explained my move to her."

"When you've got the new one in your pocket, put the battery back in and we'll buy it on a ride in some taxi cab. Lief will have a moving target to track."

My opinion of Doug rose a full ten points.

"Usually, only law enforcement types are able to track a phone — or helicopter moms who've installed a stalking app. Does your ex have contacts with the cops or is he smart enough to mess with your phone?"

She laughed, "Not hardly."

Jakup and I glanced at each other, the same thought at the same time. *These a-holes he's been hangin' with must've gotten into an NSA database and lifted her location. NOT good. "*

The head part of Doug swung our way, one eyebrow lifted in a question. Jakup's head bobbed and his beak clacked. From past experience, I knew the clacking took concern to a whole new level. Doug's visible shoulder slumped.

Hillary was not blind, nor was she dumb. I guessed she'd realized toot sweet how big a bind she was in. Lief as part of a skillful gang of conspirators intent on infiltrating the highest levels of government was a shitload worse than Lief, the dumb-ass ex-boyfriend, stalking her.

"So I'm screwed, huh, guys?" she asked. "If Lief is mixed up with a bunch like this I've got more to worry about than a restraining order. So what now? Contact spy central?"

"That'd be premature," Jakup answered. "Lemme spend a little time surfing on OWIS and put Betty on it, too. The phone trick is something a human would try, but Lief is..."

"A hybrid," I finished. We might have trouble on two fronts. Not good, my friend, not good."

"*Shit Partner, both our cases could blow up on us big time. Did we bite off more than we can chew?*" I mindsent.

"*Half of this mess is because you got the hots for Hillary.*"

"*Big talk from a feather lech.*"

His beak clicked.

"*On the bright side, J&R is better than the average bear. Between us, we've got some skills and, if we play 'em right, I think our clients will be more help than hindrance.*"

"*Umm.*"

Then Hillary's phone vibrated. The room went dead silent.

CHAPTER ELEVEN

"Don't answer it," I said. I was too late—by force of habit, she'd pushed "accept." A split second later, she realized what she'd done and dropped the phone.

"Wonk," sounded from the floor and the lights went off, the TV silent. Six sets of eyes focused on the deadly rectangle. The last set dive-bombed the phone and stood listening to the voice coming from it. His head popped back up before he hopped on "end."

"Your dry cleaning is ready," Jakup reported after listening to the recorded voice.

"Well, I would hope so—I dropped off my stuff three..." she began, then realized how ludicrous she sounded. " I mean...what a relief. What if it'd been Lief again?"

"We could assume he'd found our exact location," finished Doug. "And that would not have been a good thing."

"Yeah, but why'd the lights and the TV go dead? What if..."

Then the lights came back on and the TV delivered a jingle about poi, the perfect finishing touch on your Hawaiian plate.

Yeah, like I believe that. That stuff might do a good job of gluing together a couple cracks, but eat some? No thanks. Leave that crap to the tourists at their make-believe luaus.

"Who knows? Maybe a lava flow took out a substation—or one of my relatives landed too hard on a transmission line. Probably not enough left for a funeral," Jakup answered with the movement I'd learned was the scrub jay equivalent of a shrug.

"Nice thought, all-knowing-one, but, just to be safe. How 'bout I 'port us over to the other side of the island. I hear Penelope's House of Pancakes is good for breakfast. My stomach is still on mainland time. We can go over plans there. Maybe lose Lief's tail, too."

"I could go for a bite," Doug said, "but in a dark corner, if you don't mind. Better that way."

I took that for a group yes, pictured the destination I'd surfed on my cell, and 'ported us to the back of the restaurant. If the look on the server's face were any indication, she'd have a damp spot on the back of her uniform. I didn't think I was that terrifying, but maybe she wasn't expecting two humans, one almost-human, and a bird to appear out of nowhere not five feet from her.

I ordered macadamia nut pancakes, which tasted great. Coconut syrup on Doug's didn't seem much like something a normal person would eat, but Doug wasn't normal, after all. Stomach full, I sat back content until I noticed the wooden head of some Hawaiian god seemed to wink at me.

I twitched. Hillary noticed, "What's wrong, Riley?"

"Must have been something in the syrup. I'd swear that wooden head over there winked at me."

The unsounded laughter at my expense was deafening, but Hillary played fair and turned to look at the offending face, and stiffened. "I think the thing stuck its tongue out at me."

Then she couldn't keep a straight face any longer and started laughing. "Riley, you have too much imagination. What do you think—-a Hawaiian god hanging on the wall? Really? Or maybe the head is part of a NSA surveillance operation? Granted, this place is a high-risk target where they'd have their most sophisticated devices planted ."

Then they all laughed, and I sat stewing in my juices.

"Are you serious, Riley. You are letting your imagination run away with you. We don't know yet who or what we are facing. Is Lief part of a gang or a lone ranger? Do they guard the Mark? Some kind of force field or a guard dog? Who knows?" Doug said.

I sulked. What else could I do under the circumstances? I know what I saw and no one believes me. To be safe, I snuck a glance over at the wooden head again. The thing gave me a wide grin. Why couldn't the others see what I saw?

"Ready to be an adult now. Partner?"

"Screw you," I mindsent him back."

Jakup flipped his tail at me and stalked to the center of the table. "Now—is anyone interested in what I've found out so far from OWIS?"

He used that super-saccharine tone of voice again, superciliousness dripping from every syllable. I wished I had a fly swatter.

"How bad is it, Jakup?" Doug asked.

"Worse than I thought," was his answer.

CHAPTER TWELVE

"First of all, if the dirt Betty at OWIS dug up for me on the nasties we're up against is correct, these two cases stand a good chance of ending up as one," Jakup began.

The rest of us stared at my partner shocked. "Wadya mean, Partner?"

"Betty confirmed what we suspected. The war gods have a hard—uh, *resent* how humans have taken over in their sphere of operations. Killing, maiming, the slaughter of innocents, famine, pestilence, you know the drill. Humans have been doing a bang-up job since before the Romans, but took things to a whole new level in the early twentieth century. The gods can't stand the competition and want to put your insignificant species back in your place."

"Insignif..." I protested, sputtering.

He held a wing up and cut me off. "Hold it for once, Rose. Second thing, she told me. The Hawaiian gods—more than most—have perfected body transfer with humans—or whatever convenient species they needed to use to accomplish their ends. They not only pass for, or inhabit, humans, but they take advantage of pretty wahines often enough to found many long lines of descendants. Most influential Hawaiians trace their ancestry back to some god. Still, bottom line, the war god and his various avatars were the most randy. Their diligent dalliances result in more potential allies being grouped against us who stand with the human side of the line."

"Okay, but I don't get how would Lief fit into this?" Hillary asked.

"Besides egging on humans to entertain them by killing each other, over the last century, the various war gods have been busy forging alliances with selected other species who might also hold a grudge against humans. My guess would be a certain element in the Leshy clan bought into the special brand of specist bullshit the gods put out."

"Specist?" Doug asked before I could.

"Like racist, only broader and way nastier. Their hate game covers a whole species, not just something silly like skin tone."

I nodded. The racism thing was bullshit, too.

"How does all this tie into the Mark of Camael? "

"Good question, Doug. The answer is too simple. Why? Because the gods can't call on anyone else to get control of the Mark—what's good for us is bad for them. The Mark transmits the power to see others as they really are – meaning no gods wearing a human skin would pass if the seal tablet were around. Instant exposure of the bad actors, and politicians would be out of business toot sweet. At least one cable network would fold."

"That last sounds good," Hillary muttered.

"But, this'd mean Darcy'd be able to see me for what I am, right? If we get the Mark, I get my whole body back?"

"From what Betty told me I'd guess when your ancestor traded the Mark however long ago, the power of the tablet was perverted. Once the transaction was complete, the corruption resulted in your species becoming diaphanous, translucent, and not often visible. The good news—Betty's experts think if the motives of the person wielding are pure, the Mark will return to what the holders took from the wronged. You'd be out there in all your glory—buffed abs and all—for everyone to see," Jakup said, continuing, "Persons holding the Mark sense their true soul mates. According to Betty, soul mates revealed by the Mark are the perfect team – complete trust, the ability to sense what another wants or needs. You get the picture. A bunch of soulmates in a parade would never be out of step or miss the count in a beat."

"So? I asked.

"Soulmates in an army would make the Navy Seals look like pikers. They'd know who the bad guys were, who the spies were, and use their superior intuition to make the precise moves needed to take down the target," he said.

"I get it. The gods don't want the Mark. They don't want *us* to have the thing."

"Right you are, Partner. Not bad reasoning for a human. They plan to put every obstacle in the way of us finding the Mark, and will do anything and everything to prevent us from taking possession."

Doug's head sank down to where his knees must have been. "I'll never have my darling Darcy."

Sometimes Doug sounded like such a sap.

"One more thing—from our opponents' perspective the most important thing, with proper encouragement, the Mark broadcasts pure love and forgiveness. The last thing these clowns want to do is let an inferior species such as yourselves bring them down without a fight. And that, my friends, is why they want no one else to retrieve the Mark of Camael. They'll either destroy the tablet—if it'll let them—or dig a hole so deep no one could get it back. Blam—no more peace, love, and happiness on this planet, maybe more damage."

"Sounds good – we get the Mark, Doug gets Darcy, and California gets rain again."

"Not so fast partner. I haven't shared the flip side yet."

"Gods assuming human form and threatening us with every other nasty species isn't enough?" asked Hillary.

"If we fail, assuming we survive, the other side will take over. Scorched earth won't even come close to describing our world. Those folks expecting to ascend to heaven after Armageddon will have another think coming. Bye, bye harps and wings."

The temperature of the air in the room sank about a hundred degrees. Engrossed, we stared at each other. Jakup and I'd stepped into something big time. Hoo boy.

"And all we can do in the meantime is have Riley flit us from one place to another to avoid getting caught by Lief or his buddies—great," asked Hillary.

"That's pretty much it unless we pin down the location for the Mark and put things right," Jakup answered.

Holy shit.

"We need to get out of here and go someplace safe," said Doug.

My perfected psychic instinct sensed someone creeping close to our table. I turned. The intruder had slitted green glowing eyes. Not good.

CHAPTER THIRTEEN

C'mon now—I'm no illiterate dummy. I read *The Jungle Book* so I knew as soon as he/she opened his/her mouth what the creature was.

"Ssssam isss on break. I'm Dante. Do you wisssh anything elssssse, or sssshall I bling your check?"

Snake. Part snake, anyway. And its accent says it came from somewhere in Asia. I kind of remember the people who spoke Chinese couldn't pronounce R's and the ones who spoke Japanese blew their L's—or maybe the other way around. Whatever. *"You need to find out what the hell she/he/it is, Partner. Like maybe a clue why a snake's here playing server at a pancake restaurant."* I mindsent Jakup.

He assumed the cocked head pose he used when connecting to OWIS, and, a few moments later, he mindsent me back what he'd learned. *"Betty thinks she/he's probably Yuan-Ti. They're a nasty half-human half-supernatural snake being. Yuan-ti are sly and calculating, and they're always working their own hidden agenda. Their human side seems slick with an oily charm—-suave enough to run con games. As a species, they've no objection to forming alliances with other evil creatures—or even humans. They regard working with lesser species as a way for the Yuan-Ti to meet their own objectives."*

No one else seemed to notice anything different about Dante. Hillary and Doug appeared totally oblivious that a six-foot snake stood not two feet away. *How come I was the only one who saw this creature its true form?*

Jakup overheard my thought. *"Dummy, you don't. You're picking up the thing's self-image of from inside its mind. You're psychic, remember?"*

Did he always have to be so freakin' sarcastic? And right so often?

"Just the check," I said. "Unless someone wants dessert?" I added glancing around the table.

Hillary shot me a pitying look, "Most people don't order dessert at breakfast, Riley, and, besides, your entire meal would qualify as dessert."

Holy cow, was Hillary somehow channeling Mom? Another witch in my circle? That was exactly what Mom would say—even the tone of voice was perfect. What if she were? Probably not, I realized. If she were like Mom, she'd already know I needed to get a protection spell to apply around the perimeters of our classy digs at the Fairmont and would have one to go in the side pocket of her cargo pants. Not happening. The tone of voice was right, but the talent was different. Aloud I said to the snake, "Guess not. Just the check."

"Ask him what the hell he/she is doing here," Jakup mindsent me.

"Ask him yourself, Hotshot."

"I tried. Either he's blocked or our minds are too different to mesh."

"And you think I can better relate to an overgrown snake because…?"

"You're always bragging on how you're a world-class psychic. So world-class away."

I tried, with success, of course, but I gotta admit I hadn't been in a mind this ugly since I'd encountered the wisps who kidnapped that teen troll Merilee. The Wereweasel case came close, but this thing, whew. Icky.

"Why're you here? I thought they only hired snakes as busboys."

The Yuan-Ti's head snapped my way. *"You can ssssee me? What are you – you can't be human. They can't ssssee ussss for sssshit. The gods got you ssssspying on ussss?"*

"What makes you think I'd be working with the gods? Can't you tell I'm human?"

"Duh—jusssst because ssssomething ssssmellsss like a human, ssssoundsssss like a human doesn't mean it is. Sssssome of thosssse foreign godssss infesssssting our island might ssssstoop even that low if the sssssstakes were high enough."

My arm muscles tightened, pre-punch. I half-stood, but Jakup called me off. *"Sticks and stones, Partner. Maybe we can pump him for intel on what the gods are planning."*

"What's this we stuff? You got a parasite?"

His talons dug into my shoulder—his not-so-subtle hint for me to get back to business. Sometimes being a world-class psychic sucked.

"Let's have it, snake. You've been following us. No reputable place hires a snake for the wait staff. Maybe you're working for the gods."

"Naw, we've got a long ssstanding truce with the native gods, their avatahs and all thosssse greedy basssstahd newcomersssss want usssss out of the picture sssso to be flee do their thing."

"What thing?"

"The usssual – world domination, sssssubjugation, and wrolesssssale muhdah. Not that we got anything against thosssse if they didn't act like they'd put ussss into the ssssubjugated class. We'd have no problem if the asssssholesss ssstayed where they belong– but musssscling in on owah own backyahd pissssd usssss off.'

"What makes you think you'd have a chance against 'em anyway?"

"We can handle ourssssselvessss. You're the onessss who need to watch youah backssss. Probably the reason yuah here. For what it's worth—the lumor is theyah after some talisman hidden in one unlucky Ilandah's backyahd with the power to sssabotage their plesssent and future plansss. We've got sssskin in the game 'cause when a world loses more peace and love, trust goes out the window—no more gullible slobs'd wreack havoc on our ussssual cons."

"You're a con man."

"Don't get insssssulting, human. We ah sssso above a con man."

"Any idea where this peace and love thing might be?"

"Ssssssso you could give it to the godsssss? Hell, no."

"Giving 'em the Mark is not what we had in mind. So you do know."
"Not know. Have a clue."
"Yeah, I'm listening."
"What askssss but never anssssahsss."
"That's it? That's your clue? A bloody riddle?"

CHAPTER FOURTEEN

The snap, snap, snap of Hillary's fingers in front of my face startled me.

"What the ...?" I began. She was bending over, and her face was less than a foot away.

"Wake up, Riley. Wake up. You've been staring into space for the last five minutes. Not answering anybody. Are you okay?" she asked.

I glanced over at her then at the clock on the wall. Holy cow, she was right. The Hawaiian god's head next to the clock smirked at me and crossed its eyes. "Where's our server?"

"He couldn't just stand around waiting for you to say something. He said he had another table," Doug answered. "Why?"

"That guy wasn't what he seemed. You didn't see him as I did. If you had, you'da all freaked. Not many vertical six foot snakes around."

"What are you talking about? That guy was no snake."

"Sorry, but he's right," Jakup said, breaking in. "What'd you learn? Anything?"

"Yes and no. Make that a little yes and a big no. He gave me a clue where the Mark might be, but the clue was a freakin' riddle."

Jakup straightened, alert. "What was the riddle? Do you remember the exact words?"

Like I wouldn't? Get real, bird.

"What asks but never answers?"

"What's the answer?" Doug asked.

"No answer, he never told me. That's the big no. He claimed he'd heard a rumor about some kind of hidden talisman, and claimed was a clue about where or how to find the hiding place."

"Well, I sure don't have a clue about your clue," Doug said in exasperation.

"And the Yuan-Ti are known to be devious," my partner added.

Some general head shaking ensued, but my gut said the hissing huckster had given us legit intel. From my brief time in that garbage pit of a mind, I'd learned this was one sneaky son of a bitch who'd sell his brother out if the price were right. I also was aware—like Jakup said—their whole species were double-dealing con artists out for their own ends. The sincerity surrounding his so-called hint seemed such a contrast to most of his conniving memories. I figured our effort to follow up would be worth the trouble.

Hillary wasn't convinced, and she didn't see how chasing a nonsensical clue would help her ditch Lief. "Are you always into chasing geese?"

"What's some clunky bird gotta do with this?" I asked.

"Figure of speech from the Midwest, Rose. Move on," said Jakup.

Hmm, what would they say here? Nene netting at night?

"Whatever," Doug said, sounding assertive for the first time since we met. "If the riddle is credible, I've got a few ideas we should check out. By the way, Hillary, did you forget your Lief was mixed up in the gods' caper?"

Uh oh, dissent in the crowd.

"No I didn't, but, get real, why should we waste our time chasing a kiddie humor clue?"

Jakup and I eyed each other.

"*Double fee on this one, Partner,*" he mindsent as a reminder why.

"*I don't think the snake slanted the story.*"

"*Then we go for it.*"

"What's your idea, Doug?"

"Actually, I've got two," he said. "Either the big Tiki statue on the Kona coast or a carved grave marker in one of the cemeteries."

Hillary's crossed arms and body language said, "Bullshit."

"Why?" she asked.

"People are always asking questions at a gravesite and not getting answers. Ditto for the Tikis—talking to them, challenging them, why not ask one of them?"

"Not what I'd call a close connection," Hillary said. "I talked to my cat back home, too. She never answered. She'd rather poop on my bed and scratch the litter all over the floor."

"Have you got a better idea?" I asked, trying to slow her down.

"Other than forgetting this silly riddle idea, no."

"Where's the closest graveyard or the most famous? I asked, trying to ignore her bad attitude.

"I saw a tourist information stand down the road. We can stop by there," Doug said.

Hillary stood up, hands on hips, and said, "If you're serious about this riddle thing, I guess the Pu'uhonua O Honaunau National Historical Park would be a good place to start. If the Mark brings peace and love, the City of Refuge in the park would make sense—assuming any of this is plausible. Back in the days before the missionaries messed up the local system, anyone who'd committed a kapu on the person of a royal would try to flee there to avoid being put to death."

I stared at her. Kapu? City of Refuge? This sounded like pure bull-pucky. Now, who's the kidder?"

"How do you know all this?" asked Doug.

She turned in his direction. "The simple answer is when I first came here, I played tourist. I visited every island, went up to the top of Haleakala, down the road to Hana. I tried to surf the north coast of Oahu. I even sat in on a class about the Hawaiian religion but got so confused, I left at the break. I wanted to know all I could about my new home and tried to blend in with the natives. I thought knowing the island and the people would give me cover. I worried Lief would show up asking about me—my mom was my major news source. Every time she'd been with someone who knew him, she heard something about what Lief had said—stuff along like 'how he was going to f*ing get me for leaving,' or how he'd 'show me my place.'"

Her obvious fear hit me as hard as the fly ball I'd taken right in the gut in the fifth grade. The break in her voice left a deep silence in the room.

"Uh well, good for you. Be prepared—that's the thing. When I need directions on the Island, I'll know who to ask."

To break the tension, I picked up the whole bunch and 'ported us to the middle of the village I'd discovered in her thoughts. Here to there. POW. Just like that.

CHAPTER FIFTEEN

I made what a pilot might call a hard landing—aka a controlled crash— on a stretch of the over-heated white sand. I put us down ass first and wished I'd taken time to reread the chapter in "Teleporting for Dummies" where the author'd covered levitation. If I'd been lucky, I'd not end up with a bright-red baboon butt. A double-bun sunburn was no joke.

"Everybody okay?" I asked.

"Not dead," said Hillary. "At least I don't think so. Although the sun up there puts out enough sizzle to fuel the oven they use to heat hell."

"How would she know what hell's like? She's no demon," I mindsent Jakup.

"Get real, Rose. She's using a metaphor."

"I knew that."

"You're right, Hillary. The choice is get in the shade or get fried," Doug said.

Like he needs to worry with only a third of him showing. I glanced around and spotted this pointy-roofed fort a few hundred yards away. Chances were good we'd score cover inside. I pointed at the log stockade guarded by what appeared to be a two-platoon force of Tiki statues on the perimeter. "Let's head to Fort Tiki."

Jakup led the way, and the rest of us trailed after him. The hairs on the back of my neck stood up—yeah, I know that's overdone, but sometimes the trite is right—and I felt eyes from unseen observers following us as we trudged toward the fort.

"We're not alone, Guys," I said. "I can't get a handle on who or what they might be, but we're way too interesting to something—or something—for me to feel comfortable."

Hillary glanced around and shook her head. "I think you're imagining things, Riley. Look around—we're practically the only ones here. Until they finish repairing the seawall, the Park Service only allows limited visitors. "

"I don't think Riley is referring to tourists," Jakup objected. "I checked this place out when you suggested we come here. Betty, my OWIS contact, told me the locals believe lost souls float around the walls–they're the remnants of those who weren't successful in reaching the village. Don't forget, Riley's had enough interspecies communication to make him sensitive to other-than-human beings. He might not be picking up ghost vibes, but odds are he'd be right about someone or something monitoring us."

The chilly auras circling us weren't human, at least not anymore. I'd never met a ghost, but if these weren't members of the undead, I'd be a pig's patootie. As soon as the thought crossed my mind, I caught a series of white lights streaking by in my peripheral vision making Doug visible if only in a flickering strobe light kind of way. The flashes triggered my barf reflex. The best I could do was to run over and pop my cookies at the base of the nearest tiki. I could handle ghosts, but the other hostile things wanting in on their play posed an open question. When I stood up and wiped my mouth, the eyes of every tiki seemed focused on me. Talk about creepy.

"If you're not feeling well, Riley, why don't we finish up what we came here to do and get back to the hotel so you can take something to settle your stomach," Doug suggested.

"We're already here, and we might as well not make another trip. I think we need to figure out where the tiki for Lono might be. She'd be our best bet for an answer, seeing, as she's the goddess of peace. My guess is she'd be less enamored with the war gods plan and more likely to help us," Hillary said.

"Excellent suggestion, Hillary," said Jakup flippin' on the switch to activate his major suck-up mode.

Doug turned slowly and replied, "I see oh a hundred or so tikis here. How are we supposed to find the one for Lono?"

"Look for the one with boobs," I said.

Hillary shot me the look. So what did she expect me to call those things? Mammary glands?

"Makes sense," I continued. "If we were looking for a guy god, we'd check...."

"We get the picture, Riley," she said turning toward the Doug part. "Are all guys this crude?"

"Of course not. The term we in the lab would use depends on which portion of the breast you might wish to reference. The muscle is the gluteus, then there're the milk glands also known as mammilla, and the rest is pectoralis. A boob is quite a complex organ."

Once a nerd always a nerd. Good to know, though. Next time a self-admiring beach bum talks up his pecs, I'll ask him if he has some kind of hooter obsession.

Jakup left to do an aerial surveillance of the place. Good idea. I'd make the trip from place to place faster, but nothing's better than a flyover to pinpoint where something might be hiding. Think drone.

"I think I spotted the one we want," Jakup said when he returned. "I flew over several smaller females, but the major female tiki stands near the seaway."

"Perhaps before we leave, we should each take a palm frond for shade," Doug suggested.

"Great idea, Doug," Hillary said, giving him a big smile.

Why's she coming on to him? He's a nerd and already taken.

I let the other two find their own frond, but I 'ported a big one for me from outside the compound. We'd gotten about halfway when coconuts started dropping—thump, thump—and the seagulls attacked from both flanks. The nearest tiki had a big smile on his face.

An *Uh oh* crossed my mind a second before I biffed it and hit the sand with a thud. Something had buried its teeth in my leg.

CHAPTER SIXTEEN

In no time flat, I went from being their big brave guide to a rolling-in-the-sand-idiot. After I caught my breath and could twist around to check out my leg, I discovered several gaping puncture wounds on both sides of my calf. The good news was I didn't see any blood dripping down my leg, but spots showed on my shoes. Weird.

Blood or no blood, the bites hurt like hell. My attacker was barely visible. I spotted the translucent large white dog with the big canine teeth before he charged and tried to rip another pound of my flesh away. My dodge and swat maneuver was successful. I squelched my momentary suspicion somehow Doug'd smuggled a dog along—which didn't make sense since I'd provided transportation over from the mainland.

His mastiff shape seemed to fade and rematerialize in waves. Great, the other possibility was a ghost dog. What next?

I kicked out with my other leg, grabbed a nearby-big black rock—basalt, if I'm remembering my Geology 101 rock stuff right—and pounded at its head. Dumb move, I suppose, but I guess the ghost-thing didn't realize a rock wouldn't be able to do any damage and reacted the same way as a living dog would. The in-and-out dog-form yipped, backed-off growling, but kept a safe distance away. The bad news. Not a single sign of any damage on the beast, but I jumped up, waved my arms, and made aggressive shooing motions. The creature turned tail and ran.

Neither Hillary nor Doug saw the dog, of course. They seemed convinced I'd either had some kind of sun-induced fit or I'd lost my marbles. Either explanation would do. They stepped back in case I got violent. Jakup hovered over their heads and explained. "Riley was just the victim of a ghost dog attack. Betty at OWIS mentioned we might run across one or two here. They're long-dead warriors trapped in the area as dogs. Something about they're having been cowards in battle. My partner beat the miscreant off, but judging from the bites on his leg, we need to get our business here done PDQ. Some doc should look at the wounds. Hopefully we won't have to find a supernatural physician."

What's with Jakup and his using big words no one understands? Scrub jays think they're so hot.

"Yeah, someone should. They hurt like hell," I said, "Agreed, and another thing—the less time we spend here, the better. Not many friendlies around."

Hillary came over and put her arm around me, checking out my leg. "Jakup is right, Riley. Your lacerations are severe, but I don't have my bag with me."

Bag? What bag? Oh yeah, she's a nurse practitioner.

I made like an invalid hoping she'd keep the arm where she'd put it, but, no luck. I couldn't win for losing today. She stood up and glanced seaward. "How far to this Lono thing, Jakup."

"Not far, not much more than the length of three or four soccer pitches as the crow flies, I'd guess."

"Okay, you ready, Doug?" she asked. He nodded.

"Riley, I'd suggest you grab a stick to support that leg."

"Hey, wait a minute, who's running this show?" I mindsent Jakup.

"Chill, dude, ya never want to discourage a volunteer."

"Right you are—especially one soft and curvy."

I'd been a master drama queen when I played soccer back in middle school. No one on the team was as dramatic at faking a foul. Fall back, grab the head, twist and groan, peek at the official under the elbow. I was a sports thespian par excellence. I pulled out all my acting skills as I hobbled down toward the beach, leaning into Hillary for support, and inspiration, but I may have overdone the groaning act a bit—either that or my arm draped over her shoulder may have slipped down too far.

"Riley, you are heavy. I know you're having some pain, but you need to straighten up and put the stress on your other leg," she said. Subtle, neutral words, but her wrinkled eyebrows and sideways glance said, "Keep your hands where they belong, Riley Rose."

"I'm sorry. I didn't realize..." I said. Like hell, I didn't.

I wasn't fakin' the hurt—the path to the seaway seemed a long way away. I was afraid we weren't moving because the size of the girl-tiki's head didn't seem to get any larger as we approached. Damn, she was big.

Jakup, per usual, tried to steal the limelight and hit Lono with our question first. She didn't bite, instead, her eyes rotated in my direction. Sometimes I surprised myself with my inter-species communication abilities. Not that she technically was part of a species, more like a giant wooden salad fork, but still.

"Great goddess," I mindsent, *"we are here on a great mission and seek your assistance in finding the object of our quest. The war gods have aligned against peace and prosperity, and we strive to thwart their dastardly schemes. Can you answer one question for us?"*

I half-bowed, guessing this is what one did with goddesses. She didn't seem much impressed with my extra effort. One mongo-shoulder rose slightly.

"Ask," she commanded.

"What asks but never answers?"

"Look, buddy, ordinarily I'd love to help you, but come on ...you're bothering me with a riddle?" she asked in an exasperated tone.

"A somewhat reliable source gave us this tip. Whatever insight you might be able to shed for us would be most welcome."

"What a line of bullshit," Jakup mindsent.

I pretended not to pick up his thought and waited. The tiki was silent. I stared back at her. A couple seconds later, a small bird I'd not noticed sitting there squawked and dug its talons in her shoulder. Until the critter screeched, I hadn't realized the smallish-feathered lump on her shoulder was alive. I'd figured the bird was part of the statue. Not so, he acted like an island version of an urban pigeon.

Lono's gruff voice entered my head again. "Above my paygrade, mortal. The wise question you pose does resemble, in an inane way, the lore of the ancients, but as to the meaning, I don't have a clue. You must seek your answer elsewhere. Solving the riddle must be a big deal, though. You are the second bunch here today."

With that, she sunk back into rigidity.

Crap. The *second*? Now what do we do?

I stepped back and sat down on a nearby boulder to take the weight off my aching leg. "No luck, guys. Well, that's not true—bad luck we got. According to Lono, someone else's been nosin' around. What now?"

"Lief,"Hillary whimpered in a frightened tone.

What could I say?

"Maybe," Jakup said. "No doubt now we've got competition."

Our little circle stood motionless and silent, which was why I didn't move when the bird on Lono's shoulder took off, dived bombed me, and nailed the top of my head with a squishy white message filled with feathers.

CHAPTER SEVENTEEN

"Friggin' pigeon wannabe," I yelled, shaking my fist at the bird shape fading in the distance. Talk about your wounded warrior—crouched, eyes focused skyward, gouged by big bites marks on my leg and bird poop on my head. I glanced around hoping to find an abandoned piece of tissue. Who cared if someone'd used the wad once before—couldn't be any worse than what I was wearing.

I felt a tap on my shoulder. Doug's arm and a hand emerged and held out a cluster of Kleenex. "Take this before you start to stink," he said, with too much satisfaction clear in his voice. Like, what had I ever done to him? We agreed to take his case, didn't we?

I scrubbed at the disgusting mess mixed in with my hair. I fished what seemed to be the last bit into the tissue and looked down to see how much. "Hey, Jakup, wadya think about this. Bird to bird, so to speak. This shit doesn't look like any of the bird crap I've ever scrapped off my car. All kinds of weird stuff in it."

Jakup was not amused. He leaned over and peered down from his perch on my shoulder. "I'd say obsessing over dung is more of a Doug thing, but I can tell right off. That's not from an ordinary songbird or a corvid like my relatives. Wanna take a look, Doug."

Doug put his head down, stared at the mess, and then bent to sniff the stuff. YUK. My left nostril curled. "Jakup's right. My guess is some kind of predator bird—like a hawk or an owl. The specimen is remarkable in the diversity of the composition."

These science geeks are one weird bunch. I couldn't imagine getting my jollies over sniffing bird droppings. To each his own.

"Why do you say that, Doug? Hillary asked.

"Usually, we'd only see remains of one prey. Riley's...uh...stuff had bits and pieces of several including one I don't remember being on this side of the island. That little guy gets around, apparently. Odd place for him to perch, too. On the tiki, I mean instead of a more secluded spot. Not in character for his species to be so exposed."

Then Jakup does his know-it-all act again. "Let's not get off track. We're on a mission. After Riley gives us a break and spends time under a beach shower, we need to move on."

"Cemeteries, right? Ones with statues," Hillary said, her fingers already caressing her phone surfing for possibilities.

"Put me down under the 'this search ranks as nothing more than a snipe hunt,'" Doug said. "Pursuing silly child's doggerel is a distraction."

"You have another suggestion?" My partner asked in his world-class, snide sarcasm tone. "We know what we're looking for and why we'd want to lay our hands on this long-lost object—which, if I remember right, is getting you back together and on your way to marital bliss. What we don't know is where we need to search. What's your idea instead—Google Street view?"

"The riddle is all we have to go on now, Doug," Hillary said. She turned to face Jakup and me. "If you're on a roll with ideas, how about telling us why Lief would hang around with the war gods?"

"Specist bull..." I said, recalling my partner's previous explanation, but Jakup interrupted me.

"I got this, Riley. Lief's part Leshy. Hillary, you said he'd changed after his visit. The polite way to describe a Leshy is a woodland sprite, but a better way is forest demon. He grew up with his human side in control, but something must have called up his demon nature. The one thing the Leshies want, need as a species, is the forest. If the war gods convinced 'em humans were the persons responsible for the destroying of the world's woodland, with his mind already polluted with bigotry, he and his fellow Leshies might figure they'd hit the perfect trifecta—protect the woods, rid the earth of pesky humans, and reign as kings alongside the war gods. No one ever said Leshies were the sharpest tools in the shed. What they bring to the game—from the gods perspective—is their remarkable ability to shape-shift, which would serve the gods well for surveillance and intelligence gathering assignments."

"That means us getting the Mark of Camael would solve both of their problems," I said, waving a hand at our clients. Sometimes Jakup's long-winded explanations get out of hand.

"I'd be whole again."

"Lief might be back the way he was when we were together."

I didn't much like the getting back together part. "Yeah, yeah, moonlight and roses. Captain Obvious speaks. Don't forget, we have a job to do. We struck out here. Where next?"

"Well, either Lekeleke Graveyard, Alae Cemetery, or Laupahoehoe Cemetery. Laupahoehoe is the closest."

"Lapa oi oi? I asked.

"Yes, that's where a tsunami swept a schoolhouse with the teacher and all the students inside out to sea," Jakup said in a didn't-you-know-that tone.

"I thought the Hawaiians were illiterate," Doug said.

"Only in ancient times, this happened during the Second World War, I think," she answered.

"All this is too new and too spooky," I said. "I've had enough ghosts for a while."

"According to this," Hillary said peering at the display on her phone and holding the display towards us, "Alae is not too far either. Up some kind of backroad, though."

"Like that's a problem for me." I peeked over her shoulder to see what the place looked like and what to look for when I 'ported us there. Doesn't seem all that hard."

"No, but you still stink. Shower first, then the Japanese cemetery."

I'd forgotten the birdie -pomade on my head until she reminded me. Now the odor infected my brain and I couldn't concentrate on anything else. This made me a poor excuse for a teleporter, and the angry white dog heading my way again didn't help any either.

Survival instinct set in and I bundled us all together and got the hell off that beach.

CHAPTER EIGHTEEN

I slapped on a splash of the fancy aftershave I found in the bathroom, sniffed—good stuff—and added some more before I headed to the refrigerator where I'd stowed the goodies I'd 'ported up from the kitchen last night. Better than what room service unloaded on us, for sure. I took the sandwich I'd created and joined the others lounging on the balcony drinking Kona coffee. Not bad as far as coffee goes so, I poured myself a cup.

"Strategy time," I said as I sat. Considering they all slid their chairs away, I guessed I overdid the guy perfume.

"You're over there," Jakup said flipping up a wing. "Downwind from the rest of us. Pee-yew—calling that grody aroma of rotting-rat you're giving off a stink is being generous."

"Did you bathe in that crap, Riley? Maybe even the bird poop smelled better. I'm not sure I have anything in my bag strong enough to counter that mess you slathered on yourself—and, besides, that much can't be good for your puncture wounds," Hillary added.

"Okay, get real," I said, trying hard to act adult and professional. "Have we got any new intel? News on the Lief front, perhaps? We can eat while we talk."

"Human, you're able to eat while you do anything. In my opinion, your species acts like perpetual fledglings. Mouths open all the time."

"Who asked for your opinion?" I said with my mouth full of sandwich. Then Doug butted in.

"You're not so far off, Jakup," Doug put in, going all-pedantic. "Homo sapiens appear to exhibit juvenile activities far longer than most others. The juvenile phase of elephants of some whales may be longer but they are far more self-reliant than humans at the same stage of development."

I used variation seventeen of my dirty look expression to shut him up. The last thing I needed was those two double-teaming me in the dis-Riley competition.

Jakup took the floor—actually, the middle of the table where he perched on the plant someone'd stuck there. "Yeah, both Doug and I have news. According to Betty at OWIS, rumors are flying in the supernatural sphere of a showdown in the near future. The good news is the bad guys are still piecing together their alliance. They're interested in grabbing power. The others'd want the loot. The gods are walking a tightrope—this operation needs to rake in enough so everyone walks away satisfied.

Otherwise, they'll all be fighting each other toot sweet. All indications say those of us on the other side need to move soon. According to OWIS sources, reports have surfaced describing strange incidents occurring in other parts of the globe besides here in Hawaii, concentrated along the circle of fire, but located in other locations as well."

"Ring," said Hillary.

"Ring what?" I asked.

"Not circle, ring. The circle of fire is some arty self-analysis book I had to read for a class," she said.

"You're both wrong. The circle of fire is in Yellowstone Park," the two know-it-alls said in unison. I did a quick mental calculation whether Doug or Jakup was the bigger pain in the read.

"Circle, ring, whatever, they're both round," I said. "The point is all this stuff going on shows the gods are doing some practicing on how to make everyone else miserable.

"Like how, give me an example,"

"Volcanic activity in Mexico, South America, and the Pacific—we'd expect that, but the stone figures moving from place to place and underground rivers surfacing in London and Pismo Beach. Small vessels under attack by whales. Oklahoma implementing climate change measures. The rumor mill wise guys think this stuff might be training exercises to prepare their allies for the real thing. You know, kinda like that thing in Texas with the invasion by Yankee troops."

Doug broke the silence that followed. "While you were getting cleaned up, Riley, I got in touch with a cousin of mine who lives close by. He's a world-class second-story man, so I figured if anyone'd seen any evidence of what's going on, he'd be the one."

"And?" I asked.

"Being the way we are, slipping into a party we're not invited to, is a piece of cake. Jasper—that's my cousin—mentioned some shape-shifters and a bunch of rogue Menehune were hosting a luau and invited one or two of the war gods to be the main attractions. He didn't hang around long, but he did overhear a shifter gang and some minor gods talking about making the hula instructors and teaching dance routines to the wahines. The steps and arm waving call up storms. Another set of movements turns pet animals against their human owners. Jaz had work to do up in the penthouse so he left, but his impression was something was about to break."

Work? Yeah, right, lift some Richie-rich's baubles.

"Oh, and one more thing, the gods plan to pull power off the ley lines that cross the islands and use what they extract to supplement what they need to create worldwide chaos," Jakup added.

I was glad Hillary asked "What's a lay line?" because I didn't have a clue what he meant.

"Leylines form an energy grid around the globe and one of the most powerful cross the Big Island. Sort of like stealing power from the electric company. The extra juice puts the gods in the right place to make havoc. No sweat making a jump into another dimension from near Kalani. Once hopped up, they'd be able to hop with little effort from one pyramid to another. Pun intended. Faster and quicker—make what you do look like kid stuff," he said in my direction.

"Maybe," I said, unwilling to concede the point. "Sounds far-fetched. Might make sense if there were any pyramids on Hawaii."

Hillary burst my bubble, "I read in one the books I checked out from the library that the Hawaiian translation for 'volcano' and 'pyramid' are identical."

Doug, ever the optimist, asked, "Could one of the gods be able to rain down lava anywhere?"

"Well, duh," said Hillary. "Pele is a goddess, and she's got volcano down pat."

I shook my head, but in my heart of hearts, I wasn't sure Pele mightn't be one of the war gods. "Neah," I said.

"If what Betty passed on is correct, I wouldn't rule out any possibility," Jakup said in that stuck-up-I'm-such-a-smart-professor tone I hate so much. "Time's a wastin', Human."

"Then let's get our tails in gear and head out to Alae."

I heard a "But your leg, Riley..." from Hillary and a "Stupid riddle" from Doug as I gathered 'em up and 'ported us to the other side of the island.

CHAPTER NINETEEN

I wasn't fast enough. By the time I'd put us down, I'd already felt the procession of huge raindrops trotting down my back. Even though I plunked us down under the big monkey pod toot sweet, sayin' soaked to the skin would be an understatement for us. The thick overhang of the bell-shaped tree provided cover from the heavy rain, but Jakup shaking his feather my way didn't.

"Albizia saman," said Doug, squinting up at the leaves above us. "Another immigrant to the island. If I remember right, this came from South America."

Like we needed to know that. We weren't here for a botany lesson. For once Jakup backed the play I was about to make.

"Interesting, but not relevant to our mission, Doug. We need to concentrate on the answer to what asks but never answers," he said in his evah-so-proper-and-professorial tone. If I knew my partner—and I did—that bird was losing patience.

I didn't need to dig deep to read Doug's "Stupid dumb riddle. "

"What are we looking for here?" Hillary asked. "No female tikis or any other obvious goddess types for us to question, Alae may be a big bust. Pretty, I suppose, in a quality of graves way, as cemeteries go, but my take is we find nothing here to help us locate the Mark. Or we could stay on this train to nowhere for one more stop—in other words, another wild goose chase."

I wasn't all that impressed with the place myself, but why waste a trip? "As long as we're here, we might as well check out the possibilities. Maybe that little shack over there by the other big monkey-pod might contain a clue."

"Keep us dry for a while longer at any rate," Doug muttered under his breath.

Nerd.

Armed with a rain shield of palm frond, we crossed over to the shack which turned out to be a sturdy block square holding a tittering troop of tea drinkers. Perfect. That's all we need.

"Oh, how charming," piped Hillary. "A Japanese tea ceremony. I've never seen one before."

Neither had I, fortunately.

She and Doug joined a cluster of tourists watching. Some singles, some families. One fat little kid threw me a nasty look, showing his teeth. I wasn't much excited about this tea-sipping stuff and wanted to get the heck away. My body language must have said as much. The kid gave me the finger. What a brat. Something about him was familiar, and this bothered me almost as much as having to hang around for this dumb tea thing. I liked my tea better iced anyway.

Jakup must've had a similar reaction. He leaned over on my shoulder and said silently, "*I'll do a recon flight. Maybe working from a little more height I'll be able to spot something worth checking out.*"

Good idea, I thought but didn't want to pump his ego anymore so I shrugged and flipped him into flight.

Our two clients stood enthralled by the rattle of tiny wannabe cups, the weird teapot, and the bowing, lots of bowing. Big whoop. The longer Jakup takes on his surveillance mission, the longer I'm stuck here. Fortunately, the thud of landing and the pain of talons signaled his return.

"*Couple places for us to check out, one looks like it'd pay off,*" he mindsent "*But, we might have a problem. A thick ring of woods surround this place, and I spotted several weird dudes hiding in the brush watching us.*"

"*Okay, let's get the show on the road then.*"

"I don't want to break up the party, but Jakup's spotted a couple good possibles. Let's roll," I told the two would be tea-tipplers

I overhead the unvoiced thought "*Sometimes Riley is so juvenile*" in her mind, but chose to ignore something so obviously false.

"I've got a guy we need to talk to," Jakup said as led us across the grass, past a statue of Mary who didn't give us a second glance, through a bunch of square stones to a half-dressed little dude with a disgruntled expression on his face. Maybe he was POBT because he had to wear a dress and wings.

"Waddya you want?" he demanded as we approached. "Ain't you got enough others to bother?"

Doug spun, "Who said that?"

Can Doug hear this little smartass? Since when do any humans—besides witches, of course—hear statues speak? Less human than he claimed to be, hmm?

"Me, you dumb half-there cluck. Ain't you never met a sprite before? What kind of country bumpkin are you anyway?"

Doug didn't say as much as one word. Didn't science nerds believe their own ears—especially one like him with his own fouled up anatomy?

"Chill, you look lovely, Sweetheart," I said. With its fat little belly, short skirt, and a big scowl, he wasn't going to win any muscleman contest. The rude little snit pushed and shoved but couldn't get loose from his pedestal. "If you're so up to date, I'm sure you've heard about the war gods' latest plans?" I added the question mark at the end of my sentence but didn't give him time to hand me more badmouth. "A guy back in Hilo gave us a tip on where we might track down an implement to use to make their life more difficult enough to cancel their plans. My guess is, from what you're wearing, you don't walk on the dark side. How 'bout I bounce something off you?"

"Yeah, what's that?" he asked, glowering at my crack about his skirt.

"What asks and never answers?" Jakup recited. "The clue might be a translation and not as clear as the original, but, a smart guy like you, you should be able to tell us the meaning."

"Even if I could, I wouldn't," the little monster said, "Not when some of the gods' good buddies are out there." He pointed at the clump of nearby trees. "And a couple more over there. If I open my mouth to you, I lose a couple wings and they'd smash my toes, too."

I followed the direction his finger was pointing. Not at the trees, but back where we came from. I saw that same bratty boy. A second later, his body blurred, and I recognized Lief's shape. Oops. *"We're in deep kimchee, Partner,"* I mindsent, nodding my head toward the shifter kid.

Then, overhead, the shadow of a bird. I ducked and dodged, and missed most, but not all of it gross message.

CHAPTER TWENTY

This bird muck thing was getting old. How many clean shirts did I need to 'port before this loose-assed bird stopped considering me a prime target? No question the stain on my shirt came from that same ratty-looking collection of miss-matched feathers who squiggled me off Lono's shoulder back at the beach. Wahda I ever done to him ... or her?

Despite our situation, Jakup was yuckin' it up. Doug and Hillary at least had enough sense to try to hide their giggles. *"Better watch out for the flies, Partner. Ya know what they're attracted to, doncha?"*

"Knock it off, birdbrain. Next time the pie'll be three and twenty blackbirds and one blue scrub Jay," I mindsent as a threat.

"Ha ha ha. You're so funny. I made better jokes than that when I was still in the egg."

Hillary was glancing back and forth between Jakup and me. Whatever her talent was more seemed more than random intuition. A little practice and she'd be able to pick up any unshielded mindsending. Might be good...might be bad.

"What's wrong, Riley? I mean besides—." She choked out, trying not to laugh. "One bird bomb shouldn't get you so flustered."

I turned my back to the ceremony going on and gave a backward gesture with my thumb back at them. "That kid—the bratty-looking one with the bad attitude. He let his shape slip. I think he's Lief. If he's brought a bunch of buddies with him, we've got a major problem on our hands."

Her face fell, eyes wide. She blanched, tan or no tan.

"Pardon me for a sec, buddy," Jakup said to the faux angel as he perched on its nose. "Riley's got an eye for shifters, so if he says, that pudgy person is Lief, he's Leif. As much as I hate avian metaphors, we're sitting ducks out here. We need to get to a safe place. Forget, the trees over there. I saw some tough-looking dudes hanging out in them."

"Why can't Riley just do his thing and poof us poolside?"

As much as I'd like to join Hillary poolside, Jakup was right. "Running—'porting—away wouldn't get us any closer to finding the Mark. " We need to keep out of sight, get close enough to overhear what they're saying. Maybe they'll let something slip about their operation," I said.

"I will do the close surveillance," Jakup said copping his usual haughty I-m-so-hot attitude. "As a member of a superior species well suited to blend in when we choose to do so, I will be the one most able to achieve success in an approach within earshot and learn what we can,"

"Prudent plan," said Doug. "The rest of us can return to the hotel and wait to hear what you've found out there."

Hillary gave him a disgusted look. "Doug, that's not fair for Jakup to do all the work."

He wasn't. I was the one who got us from place to place, did the interspecies communication, and all that, but she was right. Leaving Jakup on his lonesome wasn't fair. "We need to stay close enough to pick him up in case he needs a quick trip out to escape. I say we join the tea ceremony and blend with the crowd. I should be able to spot any others shifters if they're hanging with the pack over there."

"Yeah, Doug. Why don't you shed some visibility and do your part?

"I agree, Riley," she said, and slipped in closer. Worth hanging around with the weirdos if she stayed there. I puffed my chest up to seem more manly and put my arm around her waist. Damn, we looked good together.

Doug gave me a dirty look before he faced to almost total nothingness. The soles of his shoes stayed opaque and allowed me to follow him as he headed after Jakup toward the grove.

I kept a mind tag on my partner as he advanced—which was a good thing because almost as soon as he took flight he'd disappeared. Scrub jays have camouflage down pat. Their feathers looked blue, but in the right light, they seemed black or whatever their owner wanted 'em to appear. Not up to chameleon style, but better than most.

Seeing and hearing what he was hearing and seeing made tracking him easier. I got a little seasick with the quick pivots in an up and down pattern he used. None of the thugs caught on as he settled down right over their heads. They acted bored and groused about such a cock-eyed assignment.

"I could go for a cold beer. Standing here in the hot sun watching that human scum is not fun without some brew."

"Better not— any of Kukulkan's buddies catch you at it, you're toast, man."

"My luck that Hootsypuchi guy from Mexico'd be on duty and collect my heart."

"Why'd we get mixed up in this anyway? Not the safest job we've ever taken."

"No, but the rewards are greater. We get the big boys what they want, and maybe we get our own kingdom, servants, and plenty of lovin'"

"And we're supposed to do that how?"

"Idiot. Why do you think we're trailing that weird bunch with the half-seen and the bird?"

"Holy cats, Partner. They think we know where the Mark is. What gives?"

CHAPTER TWENTY-ONE

Doug must 'a suffered a nasty gas attack because the image I gathered from Jakup's mindsend which showed two of the thugs sniffing and spinning around to face each other with disgusted expressions.

"Who dropped the bomb?" one asked throwing a suspicious glance at a possible offender.

"That was one hell of an ass blaster," complained his mate.

"Havin' a party in your pants?" thug one responded.

"I never noticed before—or maybe I never connected the dots — but when Doug goes natural, you get a major pee ewe. He should carry a big-time deodorant aerosol around with him. This place smells like someone's been playing a long tune on a butt trumpet." Jakup sent. *"I don't know how long I can stand the reek. Tough on me. We scrub jays have a superb nasal capacity, you know. I tried to tell the big emitter to hold it, but I didn't get through."*

"Hang in there, Partner. The more we learn, the better off we are. Give me a holler if I need to pull the two of you out, you know, like in a hurry."

Then Jakup surprised me. He actually gave someone besides himself a compliment.

"Hey, Doug's all right. He's been going through their backpacks and pulling stuff out. He must have a kangaroo-like pouch in his belly. Once he picks something up, he sticks the thing somewhere and ... out of sight. Cool trick... uh huh...What? ... He's giving me the high sign. I think he found something. Beam us up, Scotty."

I didn't feel much like Captain Kirk, more like a Ferengi, less a Hans Solo than a Yoda. Too much bird shit on me, too many bad guys around, and not enough partying fouled up my game. If I'da met Hillary before the witches and one interfering scrub jay drafted me to be a special agent for supernatural affairs, she and I mighta had a real thing going. Not the time or the place for self-pity, but deep down I envied guys without a psychic bone in their bodies. They had a love life. And, besides, my leg hurt and I was hungry.

"Any time now, Partner," Jakup said. *"We ain't got all day. One thug noticed Doug'd moved his backpack and left the zipper open. The whole bunch is in full search mode. "*

"All right, all right, ALL RIGHT." I answered. I grabbed Jakup and the piece of space I thought was Doug, added Hillary and me and winked out. Doug was trying to say something, but I figured it's only Doug and ignored him.

"Wait, hold your horses, one of those arsewipes out there picked up a phone call a couple seconds before you pulled us out," Doug said, all excited like.

"So?" I demanded.

"I don't know who was on the other end of the call, but I overheard the guy who answered say, ' Hillary?—neah, ain't seen her. She's your bitch, you say?' About then you snuffled us up and out to ... whatever this place is." he trailed off, looking around.

I almost didn't catch what he was saying. I guess Doug'd chosen to speak on the down-low, so only Jakup and I'd hear him. "Hillary's not that common a name, and the guy was na-as-ty. Didn't want her to worry."

I nodded—relieved, their expression showed she hadn't heard. She musta been oblivious because she'd tapped me on the shoulder and asked, "Why are we here, Riley? Really? It's only a couple hours since we ate."

I gave a quick glanced at Jakup and Doug and mouthed, "We'll talk later" pointing at Hillary with my head.

"The Outback—'porting is hungry work," I told her.

Dropping in seemed logical. When Jakup sent up the distress signal to get them out of there, I figured why not? As good a place to strategize our next move as any.

Scrub jays aren't given to much facial expression, but this time Jakup's telegraphed a big-time worry. "Time for strategizing is over, Partner. The time for action has come – we need results."

We all stared at him, speechless.

"Your food fetish can wait," Jakup continued. "We're off to Lekeleke Graveyard. This was the Nine-Eleven for the old gods of Hawaii. Really big deal for them. The most likely place to learn what we need to know."

"How 'bout we order to go?" I asked.

They all turned toward me glaring. I felt like a fifth grader whose teacher caught him dead to rights.

We left. My stomach growled with disappointment.

CHAPTER TWENTY-TWO

We'd left the restaurant sans doggie boxes – not my choice. Still, I did the adult thing and googled the coordinates for Lekeleke en route. I'm an old hand at 'porting and almost never missed my target by more than a couple meters. This time I was sure I'd messed up.

When we arrived, we found this rockpile was nothing to write home about. No guy in his right mind would take his girl for a walk along the path slicing through the rock and weed landscape. Lekeleke was a downright spooky place.

For some reason, no one said a word. Hillary pivoted in slow motion taking in the scene in all directions. "This is my first time here. Everybody told me Lekeleke made 'em feel sad. I didn't need any more sad in my life than I'd suffered during the weeks after I dealt with Lief."

Melancholy, a word my Freshman Lit professor used like all the time, for once fit the scene. The wind blowing in off the sea seemed to carry bleak visions of desolation and despair. I shook myself. Some sort of psychic aura hung in the air whispering messages of death and despondency. Heavy stuff. For a big strong guy, I came close to crying. I put my arm around Hillary, and she put hers around me. Yea, Riley, you found the Silver Lining.

"Okay smart one, why's this place such a big deal?"

Doug surprised me when he was the one who answered. "The old Hawaiian culture and customs died. We're all experiencing the sense of loss comes from the regret at the loss of the life they'd lived. The last king who followed the old ways, along with about three hundred of his warriors, died here in the battle of Kuamo'o. Some say the old gods of the Hawaiian religion died that day too. Those mounds up the hill contain their bodies. Some Hawaiians choose this as their burial site. A "join their ancestors" kind of thing."

"How come you know so much about this place?" I asked, thinking why would anyone want to hang around here.

"I had a distant relative die here, killed in the final battle. My mom brought me to Lekeleke when I was a kid—Lekeleke is not a place you forget."

That's a fer sure fer sure good buddy.

The silence which followed, lasted a minute or two before Jakup made an ungentlemanly squawk and began another of his know-it-all dissertations. "Lekeleke was the old gods' nine eleven. This is ground zero for them, the end of the world they knew. No more offerings from the wahines, no more free goodies, no more worshipping warriors—their easy god days were over. A few Hawaiians clung to the old ways, but most moved on, took up the tourist trade and joined the Jesus sect. Spirits of the dead still inhabit the area, and the gods can't do much to get their jollies except foisting hallucinations on haoles who come to gawk. "

"Okay, smart bird, if everyone around here is pissed off at the world and everyone in it, why are we here? I doubt anyone would materialize to help us."

"Go "corporeal,'" Doug said. "Not "materialize.'"

"Whatever." I groaned—life surrounded by knowledgeable nerds got old real quick.

"The midday sun is a killer," said Hillary. "I spotted a bench where we could at least sit down. Looks long enough to fit the three of us. Jakup, you can grab a shoulder."

As soon as my butt hit the stone, I realized sitting down was the last thing we needed to do. The effect of the wind was bad enough, but the sensation the bench gave off swayed between fury and fear. According to the small plaque, this bench cut into the fresh scar of an a'a flow marks the place where they claim the Hawai'ian gods died. The godly ones acted all pissed over the loss, and, when I felt something like a finger up my rear. I got up—quick.

Six feet hit the ground, and we headed off toward the cluster of altars, at about the same time, three voices echoed a loud "Eey-ew." The explanation for why came from Hillary. She explained the ground under the altars held the bodies of the valiant warriors defending the gods.

The trail cutting through the area was flat and not too bad, but the jagged black rock, no shade, and blistering heat from the sun above made the climb up tough. I had enough sweat on me to salt a margarita.

"Why are we going on foot," asked Doug. "Can't you do your thing and set us up there by the tree?"

I was all set to do so when the sting of Jakup's talons in my shoulder stopped me. "We're being watched. You all need to act like mindless tourists. I'll wing up there and check out what might be skulking around near the slabs."

I leaned into Hillary like I was giving her a hug and whispered," Jakup said act like one of the mindless tourists infesting the island. Something is waiting and watching us. Somehow, we've made 'em suspicious. Jakup's going out to reconnoiter."

She put her face close to mine acting like she was going to give me a kiss. Giggled and said, "Right."

"You get that, Doug?"

"Roger."

"Go for it, Jakup" I said.

He left in a flap of wings and a flash of blue. Hillary pulled out her ever-present guidebook, and we pretended to consult the pages. She threw in a witless giggle a few times to complete our act.

She was reading something about the Big Island woo-woo stuff competed with the heavy-duty vortexes of Sedona, Giza, or Machu Picchu offered — in my opinion, this place gave the big names a run for their money. The defeat of the old ways on this bleak pile of sharp-edged rocks seemed to make this lava covered field as powerful as some of the more well known New Age must-sees. I smiled down at her and pretended to listen, but kept my eyes peeled on my partner's progress. I nearly made a wet spot when I saw the small fireball of a missile heading his way. "Get the hell out of there, Partner. Bogie at six o'clock."

He did a quick pivot and headed in our direction faster than I'd ever seen him move.

Bringing the fiery little sphere with him.

CHAPTER TWENTY-THREE

I hadn't been crazy about walking the dirt road cutting through Kuamo'o Battlefield before. The road seemed to act as a magnet for more of the disheartening layer of murky mist hanging over the area. Sad didn't even come close to the creepy landscape surrounding us. However, I could see up front where the road climbed into some scrawny trees. The abrupt color change between lava cliffs and the sea was unsettling.

Now with the blazing ball trailing my partner like a heat-seeking missile, I was less impressed. "I thought Hawaiian volcanos didn't do fireballs," I said to our guidebook guru.

"According to this, they don't," she said after consulting our Hawaii bible.

"So what's flying that thing? Doesn't look like any drone I've ever seen," I said.

Word heard from the nerd corner, 'My mom always told me the Big Island's hot spots were among the strongest in the islands. The mountain, if you measure from the sea floor to the summit is the tallest on earth. Hawaiian royalty buried their dead on the mountain for centuries, and, with the inbreeding with the gods, the summit is a psychic hotspot. I'm surprised the energy doesn't seem to bother you."

For once, Doug made sense. Maybe that girl in the lab who was supposed to be after his body wasn't nuts after all.

"You're right," said Hillary," In the class I took, the instructor said the battlefield was known for unnatural sightings. The fireball must be one of them. If I 'remember right, he called them '*akualele.*'"

"We can talk about the why's and where's later. We got more important things to deal with—like the hot little fastball headed our way."

Jakup' showed us some smooth moves—the zigging and the zagging, the pivots and reverses, the lateral feints and abrupt upswings would make any NCAA quarterback green with envy. Right now, though, I was more concerned with setting up some pass interference and getting the burn off Jakup's tail.

Time for some psychic shenanigans. I made a mental check with the proper pages in Teleporting for Dummies, rallied my psychic powers into a balloon-shape, and whipped the empty container out to sea. I filled my mental pot full of water and then dumped the contents on the sphere. I'd never taxed my mental maneuvering this hard before, but I executed the difficult exercise with my usual competence. My world-class approach, rendezvous, and dump would rival those of the best refueler pilot.

The result—a slimy green steam—stuck onto everything like a nauseating syrup. If any movie mogul spotted the muck, future audiences would see the scene as demon meets exorcist offal. Too bad, he wouldn't be able to reproduce the stink. The pukish smell would make his production and instant hit.

"Don't let that green garbage get on you. I saw a cane toad sizzle and disappear when a drop fell on the ugly beast," Jakup said as his talon hit my shoulder. "Nice work, by the way, Partner," Jakup added surprising the stuff out of me. Compliments did not often come out of that beak—unless a girl bird was nearby.

"D'ja see that?" asked Doug. "The park service trash can? The thing melted and soaked into the ground. You're not going to catch me walking over that hunk of lava."

"Riley, you can't just leave that sludge lying around. Someone could get hurt, and besides, introducing non-native substances into the local ecosystem is not being environmentally responsible."

I stared at her. I'd never heard such a long line of drivel come out of such a lovely mouth. The mouth won. Responsible coming up. "Gimme a minute--Partner, can you check with OWIS for a good toxic disposal site?"

"Coming right up."

He assumed the position and turned his back to us. Great, make time with the ladies while we've got a disaster on our hands. Why was I surprised? Finally, he spun our way and said, "Okay, thanks, Betty."

"She says the latest thing is to put the whole mess in the fifth dimension. They process in the seventh house. According to Betty, the place is on the corner of Jupiter and Mars."

"Like I should know where that would be. Did she give you a map?"

She did and Jakup mindsent me the directions. "You need to make sure you get it all. Lots of bad mojo in that green, she said."

"I get it—look, but don't touch. How am I supposed to get this out of here? Any suggestions?" The nearby lava resembled an ocher and green paisley (one of Mom's favorite words) shredded into bits and scattered to hell and gone.

The others exchanged glances. "Your problem, Partner. I did my bit."

Hillary came over and put her hand on the shoulder where Jakup wasn't. "If there's anything I can do, Riley. Just ask."

I heard a humorless grunt from Doug, who'd gone all invisible. "Maybe you can talk nice and the parts'll go together on their own. Har har har."

"Funny," I said.

I pictured the various patches, where they were in relation to the next one and the next one after that and ... I created a mental jigsaw puzzle and began to assemble the pieces. "Maybe I can do just that."

The moving muck was nearly up-chuck disgusting, but as I got better with each piece, the middle section grew larger. "Jakup, do your thing. See if I've missed any."

He took off, flipping his tail at me and was back toot sweet. "Good to go, Partner."

I felt positively heroic when I ported the patch to the fifth dimension. Until now, I'd thought there were only four.

"Now all we got to do is make sure nothing backtracked the goo and entered our dimension."

Great—now you tell me.

CHAPTER TWENTY-FOUR

The tensioned charge in the air around us was an unmistakable clue we'd blundered into someone's personal turf. Looking around the ugly rock pile, I didn't get why anyone'd think the place was worth fighting over. Maybe in the old days, but now? With a fireball yet? Was Jakup right? Did some fifth dimension intruders lurk nearby?

"What caused that?" Hillary asked. "We haven't touched anything."

"Our OWIS data points to the high probability for Lekeleke being a likely location for clues leading to the Mark. Back in the day, this was the gods' territory with psychic energy up the ying ying, and ..." Jakup said.

"And nothin' but ugly lava, a couple of discarded cabbage leaves on that slab over there, and a few hundred blades of half-dead grass around that historical marker." Mom was always big on historical markers so I recognized what the sign was.

"Those cabbage leaves are actually ti leaves, with gifts for the gods," said Doug. "And the other brave dead who are buried here."

"For the gods who got booted out of here – those gods?"

Doug nodded, "Yes, Riley, those gods. They may have gotten their asses kicked, but they're still around. The locals know that and act accordingly."
"And?" I asked.
"And the fact something tossed an *akualele* at us means they don't want us around."
"Come ooon—this place simply doesn't live up to its rep, guys. High energy, psychic shit galore, mysteries of the gods? Neah, all I see is ugly lava rocks, no food, no water, a whole bunch of nothing. Good place for a w of second-rate has-beens."

The words were no sooner said when the ground beneath us began to tremble and get hotter. Not like the nauseating slip and slide racket of an earthquake, but more like what the sound of a chainsaw might feel like. Rumble, rumble, and H-O-T hot.

"Great, now you've done it, Rose. Pissed 'em off so they're cooking up a major lava flow."

Trust my partner to put a negative spin on things. Like I intended for this to happen.

"Yeah, well, it's not like you've never screwed up," I said. "Who'd a thunk some minor leaguers would go all free agent on us? Don't small time gods lose their deity status once their worshipers are gone?"

"Once a god, always a god. Kinda like with the marines."

"What would a bird know about the marines?" I countered, not wanting to admit he might be right.

"My uncle Walt had this thing for a homing pigeon, spent a lot of time with her in WWII. He'd run interference for her if the going got tough when her CO sent her out on a mission."

"Figures someone in your family'd be in an odd twosome."

"No odder than a cowboy and his horse. They even write songs about that one," my partner said.

Time to drop this before the argument got too hot with the odd couple thing. Besides, the cowboy horse thing was completely different.

"Okay, I'll buy your story for now. Are you sure has-been gods don't turn into something else, leprechauns, or fiery salamanders maybe?"

I got the scrub jay glare, and his tail was twitching—a sure sign to back off. I'd concede this round. "Okay, they're still gods – but do they still have enough mojo to heat lava?"

"Apparently," said Hillary who clearly had been eavesdropping.

"Heating lava's no big deal for them. Some of 'em are relatives of Pele, after all. They might not be able to put out a full-on lava flow island-wide, but small patches, sure. In addition, don't forget, deposed or not, they're in with the war gods alliance. My guess, the big boys are keeping 'em busy surveilling hot sites like Lekeleke."

"Logical," said Doug, while Hillary nodded. "If my family lore is correct, the war gods weren't omniscient. They'd need someone to keep an eye on things."

The wind started to pick up and small spurts of steam shot up around us. We definitely weren't in the right place.

"Let's see how far they can go. I'll pick us up and drop in at the top of the hill."

"Good idea, Partner. If we mark the area they can control, we can probably assume the god or gods responsible are in the middle. Once we're outside their sphere of influence, we can talk freely and decide how we'll snatch the god."

"You're serious – kidnap a god?"

"Not really kidnap. Just dangle him or her until he or she spills the beans about the Mark."

"Dangle? How?"

"You'll figure it out. Now get us out of the hot zone."

I wrapped the bunch and set us up on top where there was a good view. "Jakup thinks the godling responsible for harassing us only works a small area. We need to figure out how big."

"I agree," said Doug. "Once we isolate its position, a good force field or charm should contain the entity long enough for interrogation."

"How do we do that?" asked Hillary.

I knew just how. Call in the cavalry. I popped out to draft Mom's help. A good witch is hard to find, you know. Luckily, I have Mom.

CHAPTER TWENTY-FIVE

As soon as I smelled the sweet scent of spilled beer, I realized I'da been smart to let Mom and Dad know I'd be dropping in. The expression on Dad's face gave me a clear clue –that, and Buster's growl.

"Riley, when are you going to grow up? Your showing-up-out-of-nowhere stunt made me waste a good beer, and this was a new craft brew I wanted to try. A real adult would let us know ahead of time or at least make sure the space you chose was empty," my dad snapped.

"Sorry...I...uh...didn't mean to...uh...freak you out. Jakup and I are in a bit of a jam, and I need to talk with Mom—like right away. Is she here? ... Buster, enough already. Knock it off with the growling. You aren't scaring anybody."

"He's just doing his job, right, pal?" Dad said, patting the dog's broad head.

"*Yeah, you moved out. No special privileges for you anymore, Deserter*" said Buster, the overweight mutt who used to be mine and currently claimed by my kid sister. The dog gave me a last dirty look and sneaked a few laps from the frothy puddle on the floor before wandering over to his food bowl and assuming a position *en pointe*.

"He, at least, had the right idea. He made an effort to clean up." Dad added. He never has been good at subtle hints.

"Sorry, Dad."

"In spite of your total lack of common sense, I'm glad to see you, Son," he said, giving me a man-hug. "Your mother should be here soon. What's this big problem you're all uptight about?"

Then I heard the blessed sound of the garage door opening followed by a car door slam. Mom was home. Mom, the best consulting witch I know—after I learned from the Local 723 of the witch's union she was a witch.

"Honey, can you help me with some of these bags? Too many for me to carry all at once."

"Sure," he said, but I beat him to the garage and, like, totally surprised her. I grabbed a couple bags and asked, "Where do you want them?"

"The mom in me says I should give you a hug, but the witch in me wants to know, 'What do you want this time.'"

"Jakup and I are out in Hawaii –with our clients Hillary and Doug and ..."

"Hawaii? With clients? Isn't that a bit...unconventional? What's your girlfriend say about the arrangement?"

"Ex-girlfriend, Mom."

"How sad," she said, patting me on the back. "You were together a long time."

"Yeah, well, you know how things are with me—porting off to one place or another with no notice. Really pissed her off, and she wasn't impressed with some of our clients either. On the plus side, Jakup and I have been busy. Hired on for one supernatural potential catastrophe after another. Like our current case—which is why I'm here. We're up against an alliance of war gods. We were on a site search and some pipsqueak-has-been-wannabe godling decided to make points with the big guys and put us in a pickle. We need to solve this riddle so we can find out how to retrieve the Mark and make Doug back to one hundred percent corporeal again. Once we have the Mark in hand, we break-up the war-god-coalition which is scheming to take over the world and save everybody. With no big cartel handing out goodies, our other client's problem goes away. Once the support force the gods have cooked up dissolves, her problem—named Lief—won't hang around. He'll be out of Hillary's life. *Voila*, two cases solved.

"But, right now he/she/it—I'm not sure which—is trying to cook us with lava. We think this character's powers go only so far, so if we were able to contain him, pen him in, then we'd be cookin'—or more precisely—not cookin'--that's where you come in. We need a spell, a powerful one we can use with no side-effects so we..."

"Hold on—too much information all at once, Riley. How many times did we tell you to think before you speak?"

She had a point. She had a lot. *Why did she always make me feel six-years-old again?*

"What sort of creature are you trying to control?"

"Not a creature, only a small time war god, but Jakup doesn't think he/she/it was Hawaiian originally. Maybe one of those Sumerians or Aztec guys."

"How much of what you're telling me is for sure?" she asked.

Trust Mom to put me on the spot.

"Uh—other than the attempt to char-broil us with lava? Not so much. Jakup might have more data from OWIS."

"And?"

"I'd bring him back to the mainland so you could ask him, but who'd be there to make sure nothing happened to Hillary or Doug. Having a couple clients roasted wouldn't do wonders for our resumes."

"Then 'port me to where they are. I need to know what I'm facing to create the appropriate spell."

"I thought maybe you could give me some supercharged stuff to sprinkle around or maybe a charm to say that'd do the trick."

"Riley, relying on the information you gave me would be like solving for the unknown in the middle of a meltdown in a nuclear reactor—and doing everything with a blindfold on, both hands tied behind my back, and no beakers. I need to see what I'm up against, check out the scene." She said, glancing down at her watch. "We need to get going. Your Dad and I have guests coming over for dinner."

"You got it," I said. I still don't understand why old people wear a watch when all they need to do is check their phone.

As we disappeared she called back to Dad, "Honey, you won't mind putting the groceries away, would you? And starting a load of clothes."

CHAPTER TWENTY-SIX

Back on the Big Island, two faces telegraphed their incredulity. They hadn't expected me to show up with another body in tow. Understandable because I'd been gone less than ten minutes. Jakup glanced over and said, "Hi, Jen. How's tricks?"

Not only don't people say, "How's tricks?" anymore, but I had another problem. I didn't want to introduce Mom as my mother. The last thing I wanted was for Hillary to think I was a whiney-butt always running to mommy whenever things got tough. I decided on, "Jen, meet our clients Hillary and Doug. Hillary, Doug, I'd like you to meet Jen. She's a Class Ten Witch and a member of Witch's local 723. I've worked with 723 before, and they recommended her highly."

"Hi, Jen," came from one mouth, then the other.

Hillary held out a hand, and they shook. Doug's visible hand drifted out on an invisible arm. Mom didn't miss a beat. She grabbed the hand and said, "Pleased to meet you both."

For some reason, Mom seemed to be focusing on one side or the other of me, but never straight on. When she spoke, her voice came off a bit choked. When I noticed her shoulders shaking, I realized she was making an effort not to laugh. *Jeez, Mom, can't a guy keep a little self-respect?*

Worse, she and Jakup were in cahoots. Jakup flew over to Mom's shoulder, settled down, and whispered in her ear. She smiled and nodded. Jakup had some nerve acting like he was so much more mature than me.

"Okay, Jakup says he's going to check with OWIS on a likely hometown of the god of the moment. And, Riley, point out to me where you first noticed his/her/its presence, what happened, everything you think I need to know."

"Betty at OWIS says to tell you the one bothering us is probably a cousin of Moloch, but at least several generations younger. She also says someone should place a curse on the heads of video game makers who cheat by putting real gods in their phony worlds. They screw up the records at OWIS."

"And, if indeed our current adversary fits the description, what dark powers do we face?" asked Mom.

"The guy's however-many-greats grandfather Moloch was a bad actor—demanded human sacrifice, the whole enchilada. He's is more of a second tier hoodlum—no special loyalties or realm, but one who hangs around the real power hoping to pick up work and a piece of the action. The family was of Middle Eastern origin, but Betty thinks one of the greats had an affair with a Hawaiian goddess and decided to stay. The good news is the best he/she/it can do is harass us; the bad news is, he/she/it can conjure up some major heat and injure us—well, injure you. I'd fly away out of range, of course."

"Thanks, Jakup," Mom said without a hint of sarcasm. "Now, Riley, with Jakup's new information to assist us, why don't you show me where things started happening."

Put in the game at last, no more sitting on the bench, my turn to shine. "I'll start at the beginning—when we arrived here. The first thing we encountered was the fireballs. Came from somewhere up there." I pointed to a bigger rock in the midst of a clump of small rocks. "Jakup had one hot on his tail, and I had to blast the blob to bits. Afterward, I got rid of the pieces because Hillary insisted green muck would be noxious for the environment."

"Of course, such putrid crap would be bad for the local eco-system," Hillary put in.

I ignored her and continued, putting the best possible spin on my actions. "Once the goo was gone, something goosed me from inside the bench where we sat. Needless to say, I moved us right away. Almost at once, the ground started to get hot – like lava hot— and I had to 'port us farther up. Doug suggested we might need a force field or a charm to be able to contain the local bad actor."

"Astute observation, Doug," Mom said.

His ego swelled and if I'da been able to see the bottom half of him, I'da guessed he'd shuffled his feet and blushed. *Give me a break.*

"Thank you, Ma'am. I realize Riley can put up a force field, but the effort necessary to maintain the shielding appears to drain him—plus, from my observations, the area he can control appears relatively small."

Small, huh. Big enough to've kept Hillary and me safe from Lief.

Mom scribbled on the small notebook she always carried and handed the top page to me. "Please pick these things up for me, will you? With these, I can concoct a combination to give you some protection in most places, but not in a huge – island wide— scale."

"No problem... uh...Jen, but we need something else. A repelling spell to keep gods and their cohorts out of where we are camping." *If the Fairmont can be called camping.*

She cocked her head to one side, pursed her lips, and tilted the opposite way. This I didn't need – my mom making like my partner.

"You're 'camping' in a permanent building?'"

I nodded, "The Fairmont."

"If you're staying there, why in heavens name are you all out here in the middle of ugly nowhere?"

Hillary and Doug outdid themselves, talking over each other, to fill her in on the Mark, the snake guy and his riddle, the reason why we needed to find the Mark, what we could do for Doug and for the world if we did. Mom seemed overwhelmed with all the information they shared in tandem in less than a couple minutes.

"Do I understand right –you were out here trying to find someone who might know the location of the Mark or, if not the location, what the riddle might mean?"

"That's right, Jen," Hillary said.

"What was the riddle?"

Doug answered, "What asks, but never answers."

Mom started to laugh.

"Hey, saving the world isn't funny," I burst out.

"What asks but never answers? Even you must remember some of those dumb grade school riddles. The answer is an owl, of course," she said, grinning from ear to ear. "Look for a girl owl, the females are wiser."

CHAPTER TWENTY-SEVEN

"The shit bird—that lousy shit bird, that's who. No, she couldn't come up and play nice—maybe tell us what we needed to know and get the heck off to where she ought to be—that pokey-nosed idiot had to drop a bomb on my head to get our attention. Freakin' owl,"

Mom gave me that condescending look every kid knows and said, "Riley, I'm sure she did. You simply didn't understand, and she grew...exasperated. Owls have only so many ways to express themselves. You need to be more patient."

"You're kidding, aren't you? Did you forget my exceptional talents for interspecies communication? Or the smelly packet she laid in my hair? Twice?" I whined in a tone any teen would be proud to use. I hated the way she made me feel like a juvie punk again.

"You probably were too tuned into tiki talk, you weren't open to bird speak," she said, offering me a built-in excuse. Then the impossible happened. My partner admitted he wasn't perfect. His normally brash and belligerent voice seemed almost whisper-soft.

"My bad. I wasn't paying enough attention to a fellow avian to listen closely—although to be fair, Lono pretty much drowned out the competition. If we find the owl—correction, when we find the owl— I'll do the talking. Not that I won't be a little on edge seeing as owls aren't that fussy about who they eat."

I attempted to say, "Too bad, bird, — but Hillary beat me to the punch.

"Don't worry, Jakup. We all make mistakes. We should've time to do what we need to do."

Great—now the little bastard not only didn't hold up his end, but he's got my best bet for a long-term girlfriend taking his side over mine. Life is so freakin' unfair.

Doug glanced over at Mom. "Pointing fingers at one another accomplishes nothing. I suggest we devise a logical approach to reach our goal."

I groaned, but not aloud, because I figured one of the others would jump on my case if I did. The last thing I wanted was more nerd-speak. If I wanted a snowball's chance with Hillary, I'd need to play adult.

Meanwhile, Mom shrugged, focused at the chandelier hanging from the ceiling, and breathed deep, before she said, "Indeed we do. Riley, why don't you 'port out and collect the items on the list I gave you. Jakup, you need to work with OWIS and Hillary, I could use some of your talent balancing the energy in the mixture. Doug is the perfect person to handle placement. You'll need to go fully transparent though," she added, directing her comment at him. "Would that be a problem for you?"

"Oh, no, Ma'am. I'm pleased to do so."

Suck up, nerd, suck up.

"Riley, when you get back, we'll all sit down. You should be able to come up with a viable plan of action for us. We can discuss our options and decide the whos, whats, wheres, whys, whens, and hows then."

Now I felt like a louse. Mom not only saved my bacon, she covered for me. Sometimes having a witch for a mother can be a good thing. .

"Hillary, let's go in the kitchen area and I'll tell you what I think we need to do to create the general-all-round-protection charms you'll need. "

Hillary nodded and the two of 'em went off arm in arm. Mom must think Hillary has some talent, too. Shows I'm a great judge of character.

Doug and Jakup set up their session with OWIS. Jakup spent time putting the make on Betty the budgie again until Doug interrupted him and got him on track. *Sheesh, can't my partner do anything right on his own anymore?*

I stood in the middle of the room all alone. Everyone else had a partner. What's wrong with me? I took a shower and everything. This was like being the last guy picked for the team, the only one hanging around the DJ while everyone else was dancing, or the guy who always had to take the garbage out. If I were anyone else, I'd be in major suck mode. Instead, I glanced down at the list Mom had given me.

Whoops, not so easy. Nothing like the normal eye of newt and toe of frog, no she wanted blackberry bark —I didn't even know blackberries had bark—besom bristles, statice flowers, Dried ylang ylang petals, fresh mugwort, spider web yarn, angelica, rosemary, and mint. I googled the nearest spirit store to stock up and find out what half this stuff was. Uh oh, nearest store was Denver. I'd need a jacket if I had to be in the Between for that long.

I zipped up and assumed the position, and made the jump. Seconds later, I realized I'd landed in a pile. Big mistake, this jump. Black stinging creatures surrounded me. I itched like I'd never itched before. My first thought, drop back into real space. Nope, can't do that. I'd bring 'em with me, and they'd be attacking everyone.

My normal protective force field didn't seem to work in the Between—never failed me before. What's with this? I put as much distance from where I entered as I could tolerate and dropped like a depth charge into real time and the salty water of the sea. Let's see how they like salt water.

CHAPTER TWENTY-EIGHT

Uh oh—I forgot about the needing to breathe air thing. Gulp. Less than half a second later, I was almost out of oxygen, but I vetoed my body's survival reaction to use a scissors kick to the surface. Although I'da been a world-class swimmer if swim meets weren't so bloody boring, now was not the time to show off my skills. Now was the time for my intellect to shine—along with some help from the psychic realm.

I whipped up and concocted a quick fix by rounding out a hollowed cylinder of water molecules to the surface to bring the air down to me where the stingy things weren't. I put the tip in my mouth and tasted salt and something disgusting which I attributed to the swarm of fish nearby. For insurance, I stickied up the mouthpiece to prevent the end from slipping out from between my lips. While I was at it, I created some on-the-fly goggles so my eyes wouldn't sting as much as they were now. They worked a hell of a lot better than the store-bought kind so I decided to file the idea away for future use.

Once I solved my drowning problem, I scanned the surface above me for the enemy. The small circles on the top of the water where the creatures had attempted to follow me down into my salty space told me I'd been correct not to emerge into real space anywhere close our valiant evil fighters. They'd be an easy target for these pests. If the icky splotches on my arms were any indication, these beasts weren't something to play around with. They were nothing if not tough, and my friends'd been chopped liver by now. I felt noble.

But only for a couple nanoseconds. For now, Hillary, Jakup, and Doug were safe, but did I make the rest of humankind less safe. If their stings bothered even me, how would an ordinary human react? I needed to round 'em all up and send 'em back where they came from —whichever dimension that might be. I'd get 'em in the Between anyway.

My mouthpiece sent off odd vibrations, the kind one might expect if super tiny kamikaze pilots were directing suicide attacks at my improvised breathing tube. Uh oh, I had less time than I thought. They'd be coming down the straw at me. How'd I get rid of them— like in the next half minute?

Possible solutions spun through my mind – *swat 'em? Not an option. Incinerate 'em? No blowtorch. Poison 'em? Even if I knew what they couldn't tolerate, Hillary'd have my head if I polluted the ocean. Wait a sec. Drown them. Yup. For some reason, they hadn't swum or flew or whatever they used for locomotion down to me. So how do I get water up to 'em without them getting down to me?*

I'm no dummy. I realized I couldn't stay down here forever. The long grey shape with the high dorsal fin swimming back and forth a couple meters below convinced me I didn't belong. Now was definitely a time for killer improvisation. Figures it'd happen right after my ability to go between and 'port out to where I needed to be was most important had gone poof. I'm back in real space... What to do?

As usual, I devised a brilliant solution, not as original as I liked, more a variation on a theme. I reverse engineered the gather up I'd used with the green goo and did a gather around with my visitors from between. I devised a humongous half sphere of water just to the left and below where the stingers clustered around my breathing tube. With incredible stealth, I lifted the glob up and over the tube and lowered the whole thing over the intruders.

Of course, I took an extra deep breath before I did so's I'd not have the same issue with the no air thing. Swam to the surface, holding the water bubble steady over the spot. Back in real time and able to 'port again, I sent the container and its occupants in between. A smart jab on my shoulder told me I'd missed a couple. No problem, I did some individual dispatches and cleared the air.

I ported back to the Fairmont just as the grey shape accelerated my way.

My visions of a warm hug and a kiss evaporated as soon as I popped out in the main room of the Fairmont. My hopes for the warm welcome evaporated faster than a bowl of kibbles in front of a hungry mastiff. There was no "Oh, Riley, I'm so glad you're safe." Or "You've been wounded again. Come here so I can treat you."

Instead, I realized they hadn't missed me. Thought I hadn't left yet. I'd been gone less than I thought. "Hi, guys," I said. "I'm back."

CHAPTER TWENTY-NINE

"You've been gone? I thought you were holed up in the loo," Doug said, glancing up from the table where he and Jakup were head to beak absorbed in OWIS data.

The loo? Does the nerd think he's a Brit now? He might not qualify as a natural born citizen of the US of A —the natural part, anyway—but he'd grown up in the same country Hillary and I had.

"Yeah, I went somewhere. Was I here? No? Was I gone? Yes. Ergo—I went somewhere."

"OK, if you say so. Where'd you put the stuff Jen asked you to bring back?"

"I didn't—I got waylaid. I. couldn't retrieve what she asked for. I ran into a bad situation on the way there," I shot back.

"Yeah, like what?"

"Some black nasties attacked and tried to make a snack out of me."

Hillary musta overhead because her head when up. She left the table where she'd been assembling our protection stuff and headed my way. "Riley, what have you got all over your arms? That's a wicked rash. Do you want me to take a look at it?" she said getting up to head my way.

Does a monkey eat bananas? What guy wouldn't like a beautiful woman lavishing attention on him?

She slid up close and I held my arm out for inspection maneuvering my body so's I'd get closer. "Riley, these look like bite marks or giant economy sized bee stings. What did you do to cause this? You weren't gone long enough for this much damage. When did this happen?"

"After I went between to pick up what's on Jen's list, some big black stingy critters dive-bombed me. I didn't want to come back into our dimension and risk bringing 'em back with me. You'd all itch as bad as me if I had. So I kept going until I calculated I would be over the ocean. I re-emerged into our dimension about ten feet or so under water. A swarm of the biters took off after me. Most flattened out on impact when they hit the water. The most of the bodies sank, but a few critters survived and were hanging around the surface dipping in and out trying to get at me."

"You got those welts in less than ten minutes?" Mom's voice. "That's far too quick for something as serious as what I see on your arms—the things that attacked you — they were big black with oversize stingers? And they were—what do you call out-of-dimension— in between? We're dealing with something supernatural for sure."

Jakup flew over and landed on my shoulder. He peered down, and said, "Jen's got a point, Partner."

"Duh," I replied. "Other than expert 'porters like myself, who else would be between? That's not an especially hospitable place to hang around in."

"Exactly, in all my years with Witches Local 723, I never heard of any flesh and blood creatures that didn't need to be in a dimension. They almost sound like something a voodoo priest might call up—but that doesn't make sense either. The Big Island's not a hot bed of voodoo. Voodoo's more of a Caribbean or Southern US thing."

Hillary's face grew tight. "Southern? Oh, no! Lief told me once he had family in the swampland of Alabama. "

"Didn't you tell me Leshies lived in the forest, almost all in the north woods, not in southern scrub pines?"

"I did, but just now when Jen mentioned where voodoo was common, I remembered him saying he had some relatives who moved to a farm south of Birmingham. Evidentially they got a kick out of alligator hunting with a knife. I thought he was just joking, but maybe..."

"Perhaps not, but the stinging black things sound much like part of a voodoo curse—not a technique used by a supernatural. What doesn't fit, even if Lief does have some swamp-hunters in the family, is why Riley would be attacked. Normally voodoo cursers only do their dirty work on an individual they know personally—or sometimes if someone pays 'em enough. Why Riley would be chosen doesn't fit."

"Lief met Riley," Doug said.

Hillary was aghast. "Oh, no."

"However," the nerd continued, "To my knowledge, voodoo priests aren't quick to share their secrets with an outsider, a non-believer. Was Lief's family religious?"

"Anything I'd say would be pure guess. The only thing they seemed to value was the forest, the wilderness, basically nature. Never a hint of anything sinister...at least until...until Lief came back from the old country."

"After you dumped him, my guess would be he blamed Riley.

Her face paled.

Not as pale as mine.

"This is serious, Partner. We're a long way from the southern swamps."

"So?" I asked.

"Jakup's right, Riley," Jen said. "Only an exceptional voodoo practitioner would be able to accomplish this at such a distance. Not without help. I've never heard of such a powerful priest."

With a sinking in my gut, the answer came to me. "He did. Lief musta conned one of the priests to do his dirty work. He probably persuaded the voodoo houngan with his god connections'd he'd be able to double amp up the guy's priestly powers. Lief must have convinced one of the gods the Leshy clan was working getting us off the case would get points with the big dogs in the hierarchy."

"Most importantly," Mom said, "how long a spell did he cast?"

"Ya mean like every time I try to go in Between, I get dive bombed by black biters?"

"I couldn't have said it better myself, "Jakup said with a bit too much satisfaction in his tone. " Plus you didn't get the stuff Jen asked you to pick up so we have no way to protect you—or us."

CHAPTER THIRTY

"That's not a pleasant thought," Doug said. "I'd prefer we took measures to protect ourselves."

"Like I don't? Who's the one getting' eaten anyway? Huh? Got an answer hiding back in your lab, maybe?"

"Riley, bickering won't solve our problem or get me back in time for my dinner date with my husband. Our anniversary dinner. I've got to leave in less than an hour."

Holy shit. I completely blew off their anniversary. I'm in deep dog droppings now.

"Lucky for us, I downloaded my grimoire onto my phone. I got tired of traipsing down to the cellar to research the spell I needed."

"The entire book of spells fit on your phone?" Hillary asked. "I'd love to have a copy."

"No problem, I added a memory chip. My phone has phone-to-phone transfer capability. I'd caution trying anything other than the most innocuous spells until you have more training, Hillary. You have natural talent, but I suggest you practice with an A-Level Practitioner from the Local before you forge out on your own."

"Jen," Jakup said, "Jen, not to be critical, but let's not get bogged down in technology gee-gaws when magic is what we need."

"Right you are, Jakup. Hillary put your phone next to mine. I can transfer at the same time I search."

"Won't we still need the ingredients Riley failed to acquire?" asked Doug.

Trust the nerd to dis me again.

"I can't be sure until I find the correct spell. We have a couple decisions to make first. Voodoo spells can last forever or only for a specific time or need. We have an option or creating a psychic mirror and reflecting the curse back at the sender or use a banishing spell. The problem we face is we don't know who the specific voodoo priest is; how long she intended the hexing to last; or if Riley would be the sole or would include the three of you as well. Lots of unknowns here."

"I, for one, am pretty sure Lief is involved," Hillary said in a bitter tone.

"If he were the houngan, we'd reflect the curse back to the sender, easy decision. Considering what Hillary said though, not as likely a scenario as the god enhanced alternative," Mom said.

"Wouldn't the banishing spell do the trick?" I asked. "If I can't enter the Between, we're screwed."

"Good point, Riley. If you can't teleport, how do we get Jen back to the mainland in time? Too bad you didn't think about that and get the stuff we asked you to get," Doug said, spite showing.

"What's done is done," Hillary said in my defense. "How about if a banished spell weren't effective or broad enough? Would bouncing the reflect off Lief reverse the course of the curse?"

"Possibly—Lief might suffer some after effects, more biter attacks periodically, and occasional jabs of malediction. Are you okay with him suffering some pain? Sometimes retribution itself creates bad sad effects." Mom answered.

"You mean if I decide we should use Lief as a rebounder, I might be affected? Because I was the indirect cause of the attack? I'll take that chance. I think I'll be able to handle the blowback. I'd feel bad if Lief suffered too much, but he brought this on himself with his insane jealousy."

Good for you, Hillary.

I gave Doug the dirty look he deserved. "Like I meant to get attacked," went unsaid. Instead, I opted to play adult and said to Mom, "Have you found the spell to switch direction on the curse? Do I need to get you anything? I could put on one of those neoprene suits I saw in the surf shop. This'd protect me in Between. Seeing as I've got a good image of where the shop is, I could use telekinesis to get the suit without `porting myself."

Doug sniffed and turned his head, but I still heard his, "Big friggin' hero."

"I'll go with you," Jakup said, swelling his chest and fluffing his feathers. "The neoprene should stop most of the damage, but if I'm along, we find out for sure of the curse is broader than on Riley, and, if they're tasty, my bonus is an extra meal."

"Jakup you can't...," Hillary began.

She didn't come close to matching my astonishment at my partner's display of courage.

"Get going, Rose. Lift the suit and let's get this show on the road. I didn't come to Big Island to completely miss out on the wahines at the luau."

Island birds do the hula?

"Well, if you're up for this, Partner...I'm okay,too.".

"Simple. I ride inside the netting on your dive hood and snap 'em up through the mouth hole. They'd see the netting as your weak point. Yum, yum."

The idea of someone eating those things made me queasy, but I swallowed, assumed the position, and brought up the image I had of the dive store. "One neoprene coming up."

CHAPTER THIRTY-ONE

The tight neoprene dive suit shoved certain parts of my body up so high and tight I could not even clear my throat. Guys put these things on voluntarily? I think not.

A rising titter in the room caught my attention.

"Need all that space up there, do you?" asked Doug with a snot-loving smile.

"What?" I answered before glancing down to where every set of eyes was focused. My chest. Two odd bumps a space below my color bone told me the answer. I'd lifted a lady-suit and managed to get the bloody thing on. No wonder my package was in storage.

Jakup flew to my shoulder and poked around the mouth hole under the mesh. "If you don't take up all the space with that silly-breathing-straw of yours, I'll be fine—and any black beasties who make their way in are mine."

My stomach lurched at the thought of eating black magic bugs, but who am I to judge.

"Okay, then. You ready to roll, Partner?

"Yuppers."

"Oh, and, Riley," I heard Mom say. "Hillary and I will be finished soon. Hurry back so I don't disappoint your father. He's big on anniversaries you know."

My heart sunk. That was her subtle way of saying, "You idiot, you forgot our anniversary again and your dad will be pissed."

Nothing I could do now, unless I snagged something kinda qualifying as a potential gift at the magic store. I assumed the position and went into Between. Two seconds later —or whatever passed for seconds in the dimension I'd invaded—my hands were busy brushing the biters to one side to see where I was going. Jakup's beak was clacking as he dined.

"Hmm, nummy."

Nummy? I'd never heard him say that word. I swallowed some bad-tasting barf stuff at the thought of what they must taste like and kept going. Soon, either my forward movement or the sounds of Jakup's snacking seemed to discourage my attackers. The density of the cloud diminished enough for me to slip back into our dimension without bringing any of 'em along.

I snapped up the goods for Mom and added an Elizabethan love potion to the pile, which I planned to palm off on Dad. He's a hopeless romantic.

When Jakup and I stepped out into real time, I handed Mom the bag of ingredients she wanted, as well as the charm. She smiled at me and said, "Very thoughtful, Riley. Dad will be touched." All the while, as she was talking, she was mixing the mess into a bowl. "I need a mortar, Riley," she said holding her hand out.

I snagged one at the snooty kitchenware store on the first floor and put the two-piece set on her palm. She gave me an odd look when I passed her the mortar. I thought the pricey chachke hollowed out of an agate was cool, and I wondered why she didn't. She poured some ugly dried up things from the bowl into the mortar and ground 'em together into a fine dust.

"There," she said, moving her hands above the dust, sprinkling some kind of smelly liquid over the whole mess as she muttered wierd words. "This should be strong enough to keep away the bad guys—and I think there is enough for the three of you to put some in your pocket. Jakup, you can dip in from time to time so you are protected as well."

"Thanks, Jen," Jakup said, giving Mom a high five with one wing. "Riley is lucky to have you as a friend."

The way he said friend dripped with sarcasm. Mom didn't bite to his obvious ploy to take the opportunity to properly identify herself. "Thank you, Jakup. He's lucky to have you as a partner, too."

The gush factor was getting so thick in the room I'd need to clean my shoes. Ankle high, at least.

"Yes, thanks, Jen," Hillary said. "And thanks for the book on magic. I am anxious to try some of the spells. I won't do anything drastic until I meet with a reputable practitioner, though."

Wow, she's really getting into the witchy thing.

Mom nodded her approval and glanced my way. "Ready, Riley, if you don't encounter any supernatural headwinds, I should be back home with three minutes to spare. Nice to meet you all. Good luck in dealing with your current problems. Watch out for the red-haired god."

We were Between before I realized what she'd said at the end. *What red-haired god?*

When we emerged into real space at the back of the garage, Mom raced inside. I could hear dad complaining about how she'd cut this one way too close and why did she have to drop everything for Riley every time he showed up with some cockamamie situation?

I skittered into the kitchen and handed him the love potion. "Happy Anniversary, Dad. Use this with care."

The blank look on his face said he hadn't a clue what I was talking about. He didn't seem impressed or happy to see me, so I decided the best action for me to take was to make the space where I was blank, too. "Bye, Dad."

I went Between.

CHAPTER THIRTY-TWO

Done with Dad, I twinked me back to paradise and to the Fairmont. Lucky for me I encountered no more biters on the return trip and, better yet, when I got back, I discovered Doug had ordered room service. I grabbed a burger off the tray and sat down.

"Duds anygodi know wad Jem mend bda red harred god?"

"Riley, don't talk with your mouth full. How do you expect us to understand you?" Hillary said with a definite down-her-nose tone.

I chomped on the bun a couple more times, swallowed and repeated, "Does anyone know what Jen meant by the red-haired god?"

Two mystified faces and a double shrug said they didn't. Jakup, however, sniffed and said, "Duh, most likely one of the Nordic gods, most of them are red-haired. Might even be Odin, who knows—although why s would such a big time god want to mess in what he'd likely consider a petty kerfuffle,"

"Yeah, so?" I said, tired of his being the know-it-all again. "I get that, but why do we need to look out for any red-haired god? I hate it when Mm...Jen goes all cryptic."

"Dumb question, seeing as you think you're such hot pre-cog. Jen must have picked up a vision of a red-headed go."

"Worrying about some ginger topped Scandinavian is the least of our troubles. We need to concentrate on what we came here to do – solve the riddle, find the Mark, and save the world, and, not least, get me my girl," Doug said as he picked up a notebook and pencil.

"Don't forget about getting Lief off Hillary's back," I said not wanting to give Doug any more credit than he already racked up.

"Doug's right," Hillary said. "We've let ourselves get off track and go off on a tangent. This is so not me. I make lists, research everything before I proceed. Let's get back to business —in a logical way, this time."

"I couldn't agree more, Hillary," Jakup said in that stuffy tone old professors use. "I volunteered to be lead on the search for the owl and got distracted by Riley's issue with the voodoo beasties."

"Quite all right, that," said Doug. "We needed to make sure we were safe here. We wouldn't sleep well otherwise."

Now I'd been dissed all round—my leadership was being questioned and even my partner didn't defend me. I felt put upon and said, "Big talk, feathered hotshot, what's your big plan to contact the owl?"

He gave me what I must admit was a glare worthy of Poe's raven, scratched at the table with one foot, and flicked his tail. Jakup never scratched unless he was thoroughly pissed. To be safe, I sat down and shut up.

"We have several directions to go. First of all, Hillary should ring this suite with the protection barrier," he continued in that know-it-all phony voice he uses when he's trying to impress someone.

"I can do that," Hillary said. "I need to grind one more ingredient for the protection charm and then we should be good to go. Is there anywhere else we need to protect?"

I talked over the scrit, scrit, scrit sound the lumps made as she grated 'em down smaller and smaller. The noise grew more insistent and the stench emitted by the widening pile of crystal stuff was yucky enough to make anyone consider a good puke.

"Other than here and your apartment?" I asked, swallowing hard.

"I can't come up with one right now—but if my experience at the lab holds, when ever you don't take every precaution, you pay the price later," Doug answered.

"Makes sense," I say.

"All tight then, I'll make enough of the mixture and carry a bunch with me, just in case. Riley can do the same. I think I'll have enough to keep some in reserve," Hillary said, pursing her lips to point at a repulsive pulsating pile of crap-colored powder. We all stood around as she swept the last few bits into an old doggy-box. She reached into her purse and pulled out a handful of contact lens cases and spooned pukey powder into three. "Lucky I always carry a spare in case I lose mine. Several spares, actually."

"Indeed," said Doug.

"And I would wear that where?" my partner said, asking the obvious. "Let's face facts— the one design flaw in a scrub jay is no pockets."

One flaw? Come oon, Partner. Like that's true.

"No problem, Jakup," Doug interrupted. I can put a bit into a leg ring for you."

I was liking this half-seen person less and less. "We could call you the Banded Bandito."

Scratch, scratch, scratch. He was getting ready to blow.

"I've got you covered, Jakup," she said pulling a fat round earring out of the same place. She filled the hoop with powder, shook off the excess, and beckoned to Jakup. "Let's see if this fits on your leg."

"Like a charm," he said, admiring his fancy new look.

She rechecked the fastener, and said, "These cases should be sufficient if all we carry one."

Hillary glanced at me in a way that said stifle it, idiot. I decided to not to make the other comment I had on the ready.

"Just kidding, Partner. You might like having some jewelry, but if you tag along in my pocket when we go between to … and where was that, did you say?"

"I didn't," he said in a terse unamused tone, "but Betty is doing a search for me for habitat and using an adaptation of the Fed's face recognition program to identify the specific owl we saw on the Tiki."

A ting ting sound seemed to echo in the room.

"That must be her now," he said.

"Finding the owl and asking for the answer to the riddle, is only half our task. What if we don't understand his answer, another random chase around the Island—like every other one we've been on?" Hillary said.

"Exactly," I said. "In that case, we enlist an ally—someone who'd help us."

"Like who? Doug demanded. "Another serpentine waiter maybe? A truth-speaking cockroach? Some mynah mystic? Who?

Good question. I wish I had an answer.

"Um…"

"Betty may have found one for us on OWIS. Her opinion is our owl is a pueo. She listed a couple clues. First of all, we've learned sighting are during the daylight hours and then there's the supernatural angle. Pueos are *aumākua*,"

"What's an *aumākua?* I blurted out before I could stop myself.

"A physical form assumed by an ancestor spirit, according to Betty. They are protectors in battle and sing war songs."

Great, all I need is another supernatural bird in my life.

"Assuming Jen was right and our owl is a she-owl, she'd be our natural ally. Her protecting those in battle, probably means she's doesn't make the all-time favorite list of the war gods," Hillary said.

"Usually."

"Another good thing, according to Betty, these short eared fluffy feathered pueo-istas don't dine on other birds, they're more into small mammals. Big relief for this scrub jay. Knowing I'm less likely to be viewed a tasty morsel eases my mind. I'll be able to present our case in a more relaxed fashion."

"Yeah, more like a man to man heart to heart talk, only this'd be a bird to bird chit chat."

My comment earned me a full-on stink eye so I added, "Do I need to remind everyone we still need to find that bloody head-dripper?" For once, I had their full and complete attention. Now, if I only knew what to do with it.

CHAPTER THIRTY-THREE

"Try standing out in the courtyard with your head uncovered—that ought to attract her. You'd kinda be the opposite of a scarecrow, you be an owl magnet," Doug said in the driest tone I've heard from anyone since Professor Lovejoy in my Beginning Drama course. I'd tried out for a part in Mice and Men, and she told me I'd do better as the cheese.

"I think you'd be better at that —couple inches of bird stuff would make the top of your head stand out, be more visible," I said. "Enough bird crap on you and we wouldn't need to retrieve the Mark to make you stand out."

"Enough already," came from the chorus of Hillary and Jakup with Jakup adding, "You two are both acting like a couple fledglings who've eaten too many fermented berries."

"Whatever," I said, not being too happy at being the butt of abuse.

"Jakup is right," said Hillary. "Time for us to get organized. Racing around with no good plan is ineffective. First, we locate the place where pueos hang out. We've caught some luck—they're not night hunting birds. I hate ask you to bother Betty again over stuff we should be able to find with an ordinary search engine. What do you suggest?"

I jumped at the chance to impress her. "Our best bet would be Deeper Web. Google's okay for most things, Dogpile works, but Deeper Web goes...well, deeper."

I borrowed a laptop from the executive office figuring I'd need more oomph than Hillary's tablet. Only a short 'port and we wouldn't be using the machine long. I flexed my fingers and poised over the keyboard. I poked around several sites, talking as I surfed. "Pueos are guide birds. Supposedly, folks around these parts assume when this bird appears, they're some kind of sign. Most of them turn back if they're on a trip and later insist the intervention by the pueo kept them safe—otherwise a tree falling across the road and doing a number of their car ... or worse yet, a falling rock, which might mash everyone inside. Pretty silly idea, if you ask me."

"No, this makes perfect sense," said Hillary. "She must have been trying to guide you when she dropped her...hints on your head."

"Coulda found a better way," I muttered. "Let's see— cruises over the Waikii pastures above the Waimea-Kona mountain road ... some birds hang around the refuge on the windward slope of Mauna Kea ...."

"Isn't that near the place where they found a bunch of stick figures chiseled on the rocks?" Doug asked.

"Lemme check … uh huh—pretty close. Why?" I said.

"Makes sense ancient rock drawing, old time ways, ancient gods, owl guides – all kind of go together."

I hated to admit he might be right, but, boring as he night be, chances were he was. Dang. I pulled up a map and three large and one small head hovered over the picture. Pointing at a squiggly line "Best bet, along the trail," Doug said in a tone almost matching the know-it-all supercilious tone of my partner. "

Hillary stood up and shook her head. "Seems like more shooting blanks at the target range to me. We've been chasing around like chickens. We haven't finished point one, let alone point two and however many more we need. Let's get more on track before we all get frustrated. Riley, do you still have that shirt you were wearing when the owl dropped her sign on you? If you do, I have an idea. I read something in the book Jen gave me, about a technique for being able to —not scry exactly, but something close— to use a possession or a body part like, say, hair, to track the item to the original owner. If the spell would work, we'd save a pot load of time in locating the pueo."

Mom strikes again, Mom-lite, at least.

I strolled over to the bedroom I shared with Doug and pulled the shirt out of the wastebasket. I'd rinsed the thing lotsa times, but the stink stuck. Holding the "What happens in Vegas stays in Vegas" shirt by the hem, I laid the disgusting piece of polyester in front of Hillary.

"Put your shirt over there on the table with the parts showing the most poop up. I think Jen's method would work better with more … more traces of the owner evident."

"Make sense," I said, placing the shirt where she'd pointed and wishing I had three hands, two to arrange the cloth and one to hold my nose.

She had her head buried in the book—well, not actually, more like her nose on the screen of her tablet—her finger running down the text block in the middle of the page. She picked up a pencil and jotted down a list of items she wanted for her part of the search operation.

"Can you pick these up for me as soon as possible, Riley? This doesn't seem all that difficult, especially if we don't have to root around in the grass and lava flows."

I nodded, but excited I was not. Rooting sounded particularly attractive when compared to the alternative of going Between where I'd face a possible second round with the black biters."

I decided to try another method. "How 'bout I summon 'em from the shop?"

"You'd know what to bring without seeing an actual item or reading a label?'

I might be able to by using an out-of-body technique and then calling what I saw
to come to me, but, from the expression on her face, I decided I'd go with the tried
and true, biters or no biters. "Probably better to be safe."

"Thank you, Riley," Hillary said in a don't-give-me-any-crap tone.

"Mm ... .Jen's charm had better work, "I said before I launched into Between,
charm in one hand and intent on possible black things buzzing me.

"Oh, and a map, Riley," she called as I disappeared.

CHAPTER THIRTY-FOUR

Back in ten, I dumped my loot on the table. Not too tough, after all. The list Hillary gave me contained mostly candles—a red one, a yellow, an-orange, a green, a blue, two purples, and an indigo. She'd put a map list of the area alongside. I'd flitted in and out of some of the best tourist traps on the island, but the best I could do was a humongous tourist map of the Big Island. Photos of busty wahines and ads filled half the space making the map compelling in certain spots, but useless to any real orienteering.

Her shopping order for me had also included a photo of the person/bird/supernatural being saying it'd make locating her easier. This, I didn't get and told her, "I didn't have a clue how to get a photo of someone we haven't found."

She sighed, muttered something that sounded like "Men," as she pulled up a photo of a pueo off a site on the internet. I had to admit this was one classy owl. Fluffy feathers, big eyes, and a face resembling a kid in a fur-rimmed hoodie. Hillary glanced at a legal sized sheet of paper covered in odd pictures and scrawls, and said, "I think that's everything."

She smoothed out the map and arranged the candles in a circle around the edges. Checked the notepad. First, before she lit the red one, waited, and then ran her hands in a circle around the flame and recited something that sounded kind of like the noise I make when I've got something tickling my throat. The weirdest thing happened. As she lit each color, the flame took on a tinge of the same color at the candle. The more candles, the brighter the others shined. Pretty darn cool.

"Help me straighten out this map some more," she told Doug. He grabbed one side and she kept the other. They laid the map in the center of the candles. She mumbled another chorus of bizarre stuff and one area of the map began to glow. Hillary dangled her necklace over the section of the map, and the glob at the end grew brighter. The spot of light was so intense anyone watching would have thought a small fire was burning, the weird thing was – the paper underneath the flame was untouched, not charred, not scorched, nothing.

Hillary kept groaning and gasping out ugly words with clicks, croaks, and upchuck noises. The sounds made me uneasy, so when with a thunk, the bottom of stubby-nub coated fob hit the paper—right on top of Mauna Kea. I jumped and checked the front of my pants for a damp spot.

"Does that mean we know where she is?" I asked.

Jakup groaned. "Sorry, Hillary. Sometimes my partner is a little slow on the uptake. Oh, of course, why else would the spot attract the crystal."

"What crystal?" I asked.

"Well, the closest I could get on this short notice. This is my Golden State Warriors gold basketball necklace Leif gave me—so, with luck, Houston, we have lift-off."

I was impressed. "I didn't know you were into basketball."

"I'm not—not much at least—Lief was. I liked the chain so I didn't throw the thing away even when...when he turned into such a loser. Lucky for us, though, "she said, lifting the links with one finger and her thumb like someone would pick up a deal rat by the tail. " We know where to go, and, if this map is right, a road runs quite close to the area we want. This should make our task a bit easier, being a flat surface and all. The area shown by the crystal will be much larger than it appeared. We'll need to do some kind of grid search, but we won't have to trek forever in though bull thistles and scrub trees."

"Great work, Hillary," my partner said. "Let's go."

"How about we pack some box lunches first."

Three heads turned toward me. Six eyes in sets of two stared at me as if being hungry was some kind of crime.

"Trust you to put your stomach first," Doug said.

My partner surprised me. "On second thought, Riley is right. We'll need food and water for you earth bound creatures. I can forage, but I doubt you three would do so well if this expedition takes a while."

My stomach growled and gave my partner a high five. I was going to thank him, but thought better of the idea—didn't want to make his head any bigger than it already was. I was already heading for the refrigerator. I changed my mind and detoured through the hotel kitchen when I remembered the small sized the brown boxes under the bar. Four boxes of Hawaii's plate lunches and a bag of seeds coming up.

"Now we're ready to go," I said and bundled up the lot for the jump to the spot mountain slope shown on the map. I'd qualify as an Uber driver if I had to conduct much more of this taxi service.

No one except Jakup with his cockeyes vision saw the spot on the map erupt in smoke and turn to ash.

CHAPTER THIRTY-FIVE

"Not so fast, psych boy. Hillary was right. Close by to a road or not, this may be a tough go...and a cold one," the nerd proclaimed.

"Dude, we're in Hawaii, don't you know? Blue skies, warm beaches, palm trees, wahines in short skirts?"

Hillary glanced at me with a pitying expression. "Yes, Riley, Hawaii does have warm beaches, palm trees, bananas, and mai-tai's, but Doug's correct. If the map's right, we need to be organize how we do our search—besides flinching someone's lunch. This will turn into a sorry, cold quest if we don't consider the effects of going higher on the mountain, the colder the temperature. Not San-Diego-on- a windy-day cold—more like Minnesota in January cold—we might even encounter snow."

"Don't forget Mauna Kea forestlands can be dry and dusty in areas where they don't catch enough clouds to produce rain. No clouds, no rain. We may find ourselves on what seems like a real mountaineering expedition," Doug added.

"Why did we agree to take this clown on as a client?" I mindsent my partner.

"Probably because he has a legitimate problem— and, not least of which, enough money for a fee. I make my decisions with logic—unlike your hormone-driven choices."

I shot him a dirty look, despite conceding in my heart-of-hearts he had a point. The chance of said admission was unlikely. A quick glance at Hillary had convinced me to take her case. No reason why every one of our clients has to be first runner-up in the Miss Ugly contest.

"How much water did you bring us, Riley? Even if the temperature is low, we'll need a lot of water. According to the Mauna Kea packet, we're supposed to drink liquids all day. I imagine the former pasture areas where our owl is likely to hang out is desert-like."

"Does the liquid have to be water?" I asked visualizing a case of longneck IPA's.

"Only if you're with me," she said, sounding kinda like Mom when she told me to stay out of the cookies before dinner. "Take a look."

She handed me her tablet, which showed a landscape featuring weed-covered flat land with some scraggly trees in the background. Not my idea of prime real estate, but different strokes.

"They advise jackets, too, "she added.

"Betty says you should hone in and search for an area emitting an aura of long-ago violence," Jakup said.

"Say what? You mean psychic traces of what happened in the past?" I asked.

My partner gave me his habitual I-am-forever-amazed-at-the-denseness-of-your species stare, "Of course, Pueos are guardians during battle, so an area where the ghosts of warriors would linger would attract her."

Back in the day when I lived a normal life, I would have blown this off PDQ. Now, after dealing with some nasty ghosts in a couple of our past cases, I was inclined to go along with him.

Now, having retrieved the items on the list, I left a note for the maid I'd return in a few hours. I assumed the stance, fixed the image of the pasture and the place on the map in my mind, breathed deep, and said, "All aboard."

As I was going through my pre-flight check, Jakup caught my eye. *"We gotta keep our eyes open from now on. The spot on the map—the one where our girlfriend is supposed to hang out—"*

"Yeah, so? What's the problem?"

"I saw the area got up in smoke just as we were leaving. Some kind of warning, I'd guess," he mindsent.

"Roger that," I replied.

Jakup slipped into the pocket of my new jacket and I packaged us all for the trip Between. I had great intentions, but, on a scale of one to ten, my landing back into real space would have earned no more than a two. My foot caught on a root sticking up out of the ground creating a heap of bodies as tangled as a rugby scrum. I toppled over and the middle of my back settled on top of a sharp pointed rock. This was a major case of ouch eased only by the fact Hillary landed on top of me. Doug bounced on his butt and would have a couple black and blue cheeks for sure. For Jakup, no harm, no foul. He flew up and over the pile.

"Sorry, guys—not my best set down," I said. "Usually I'm pitch perfect."

"Maybe this is a sign we ought to slow down and get our ducks in order, arrange our owls in the right row, so to speak," from Doug.

Despite the fact he was way too proud of his clever cliché lookalike, I had to admit he might have a point. Hillary was nodding, but Jakup, in his I'm-too-full-of-it tone, chimed in, "You're quite correct, Doug. We had a roadmap to get us to this place, but not one clue to our final goal."

"Isn't that why we're trying to make contact with the pueo? I asked.

"Yes, but..."

"I told you to be extra careful," Jakup groused.

"And that would be?" I asked, ignoring my partner and not about to yield the spotlight to his puffed up feathered self.

"Locating the owl is only part one. We need information on the whereabouts of the Mark from her—which hopefully is not another rinky-dink riddle— go there, retrieve the tablet, get Doug back to opaque, and ..."

"Yeah, yeah, save the world, defeat the war gods, boot Lief and his buddies off to Leshyland, yada, yada, yada. "

"Or mend him so he's the way he used to be when we first met," Hillary said. Thankfully, she had a doubtful note in her voice.

"Piece of cake, snap of the fingers, nothing to it," I said, ignoring the put Lief back together again bit.

"Precisely," from my partner.

"Well, saving the world may have to wait, I spotted some lanky forms slinking on their bellies headed our way," I mouthed, gesturing with my lips so I wouldn't tip 'em off I'd spotted them. "*Thanks for the heads up, Partner.*"

Jakup tilted his head slightly to check 'em out. Birds have such an unfair advantage what with having eyes on both sides of their heads. "Looks like our slithery waiter and Lief drew the short straw for today and got the watch-the-interfering-mainlanders duty."

Hillary got a sneaky-smug look on her face. "How about I go over closer, show some cleavage, encourage them a bit," she said pulling down the front of her tee and tucking the excess of the shirt in her jeans. "I'd love to see their reaction when they get near the barrier charm I spun around us. I have an admission to make. I couldn't resist adding a little brimstone to the mixture to give an extra zinger to an interloper." She laughed a nasty laugh.

"I've got a better idea. How about I zip us out of here, drop down on a nice spot, and concentrate on the psychic traces of the battlefield skirmishes around here. If your theory is right, our owl friend shouldn't be too far off."

"Well shucks, Riley, what a party pooper you are—my idea seemed a lot more fun," Hillary groused. "But, seeing as you are playing the role of responsible adult, let's hit the trail."

I held out my hands and we made a circle. Jakup's talons dug into my shoulder. One deep breath, two deep breaths, and we were outta there, flitting zigzag across the area— leaving the watchers standing up shaking their firsts. Score one for the home team.

And a point or two for *Teleporting for Dummies* where I learned my levitation skills.

"Hang on, Guys, I said before I proceeded to dip and swoop— might as well make this as stomach-wrenching at Big Thunder Roller Coaster at Disneyland.

I figured my maneuvers would be fun besides providing possible evasive action if the watchers managed to catch up with us again to try whatever dastardly task was on their assignment.

CHAPTER THIRTY-SIX

Lucky me—I think I found the only splotch of softish grass big enough for four. Having an inviting spot suitable for our purpose seemed a good omen, somehow. Hillary smiled and herded us into a tight circle. "Hold hands, everyone. Breathe deep."

Without a doubt, Hillary'd been reading Mom's book waay too much. Prattled on something about merging our chakras or inner energies. Crock of crap, if you ask me. Either a person is psychic or they're not. Zero plus zero equals...well, you know.

"I've got this, Hil," I said. I didn't need this woo-woo stuff coming from the one who seemed the most normal in the crowd, but, in the end, I went along with her gig to keep her happy. Odd thing, though—when I entered my usual superb psychic state and opened to any traces of long-lost warriors, everything seemed quicker, sharper than usual. I caught hold of a weird smell and did my out-of-body thing, tracking the filament of scent to where the odor originated. The intense emotion of the place—the clang of clubs on shields, the screams, and the cinnamon scent of bravery— all hit me flat in the face with all the force of a hard-flung rubber chicken. Now all I had to do was re-enter my body and lead our intrepid band to the meadow lush with the blood of the fallen dead. Pueo central.

A short walk through mangy vegetation and we'd arrived. All the bits here fit what we knew about this adorable little raptor. Any avian real estate agent would tout this place as perfect pueo real estate – ample scrub for nesting, battle connections up the ying-ying from way back, and plenty of evidence strewn around with remnants of their favorite mousey meals. 'Now we wait, I guess. Seeing as this might be a long time, I suggest we break-out the lunches and double use the time."

"Riley, you always suggest food. Your mom must never have had left-overs when you lived at home."

"Got that right," my spill-the-beans partner said. "He might have a point though—sunset is hours away, and she won't be coming back home until the light dims. I could go for some macadamias myself."

So we munched, threw out ideas about what we might glean from the owl when she showed up, and just generally bonded. We'd all been pursuing our individual goals—Doug to reunite with his ladylove, Hillary to not unite with her ex, and for Jakup and me, to collect our fee so we could continue living the good life. Making Hillary a permanent-ish part of my life wouldn't be bad either. With this in mind, I had worked my way in closer to her, getting companionable and comfortable like when I heard the telltale splat and felt the stinky goop running down my cheek.

"You're up, Partner. Time for you to have a bird-to-bird confab and for me to pull out the big-boy wipes. Give me the double tail twitch high sign if you need me to pull you out in a hurry."

I shook my fist at the offender and waved my partner on. "Can't you ever contact us any other way?"

The pueo dipped one wing and banked in a circle with her butt dragging. I ducked and Jakup headed up her way.

"Time for the A-team to take over," he yelled back at me.

He wasn't acting all that A-teamish. He zigged and zagged his way up until he matched altitude with the shitbird. I kept a close eye on his tail. We'd blown it by not setting a mind merge before he took off. Now I was limited to bits and snatches the same way as any other eavesdropper. I'm not sure why we needed to be in synch before conducting a three-way—conversation or energy sharing, but we did.

Sure, Jakup could take care of himself, but for some reason, for the first time since we'd teamed up, I was worried. What if this bird didn't represent the good guys? What if Jakup seemed a choice *hors-d'oeuvre*? One scrub jay silhouette was just like another scrub jay silhouette. Would Hillary's protection charm work against an avian attack as well as with the black biters?

Gradually Jakup came in closer to the bigger bird, but I thought his wings might fall off. He wasn't a kick-ass flyer quick enough to keep up with the greater wingspan of the owl. I was relieved when the two headed to a lone tree nearby and settled side by side on a branch. Jakup chose the skinny end less likely to bear the greater heft of the owl. No tail bobs. That was good.

Then I began to catch fragments of the conversation. "Mark of ...Pele's....not together...ditsy human..." *Wait a bloody minute, bird.*

The two bird heads moved up and down, sometimes in unison, sometimes not. Once during their conversation, the owl made a quick...and successful... grab at a fly-by insect. I swear Jakup looked disappointed he didn't get the thing. With a screech, the owl headed our way, Jakup following. Maybe finally we'd make some progress.

I covered my head.

CHAPTER THIRTY-SEVEN

Eight talons—four small, four larger—hit the turf almost in unison. The pueo's eyes focused on me while Jakup watched both of us simultaneously. I'd grown so used to Jakup's eyes being flat on both sides of his head that the straight on owl eyes seemed off to me. I was about to commence a protracted period of wondering why when the sound of a flute broke the silence. No, not a flute, a chorus of high-pitched peeps one would expect from a tiny songbird.

"You're the one making that sound?" I couldn't help saying. "Aren't owls supposed to screech?"

"You're being unbelievably rude," a dainty female voice said in a haughty tone. "I've half a mind to take off and leave you to your own damn quest for the Mark. If Jakup and I hadn't reached an agreement, I would. Screech, indeed."

"Riley didn't mean any disrespect, Miss ...?" Hillary said.

"Wait a second, Hillary hears her? I mindsend Jakup. "She's using like real human speech."

"Of course, I'm quite capable of doing so whenever I need to," the pueo insisted. "Any *aumākua* is capable of human-style noise, albeit we of course, prefer more cultured tones."

Gaa...rate – now I've got two birds, both with an inflated ego, dissing me.

"I go by Kiki for short, by the way. Your less-than-skilled vocal apparatus will never be able to pronounce my full name. You know how Hawaiian names are."

"Enough with the chit chat, all of you. We need to take care of business. I've got a girl waiting for me on the mainland," Doug interrupted, adding in a low voice, "I hope."

I almost felt sorry for him. He sounded so, so lost. Almost, but not quite. The nerd was too annoying to deserve my sympathy.

We three larger beings took our places in a circle and the two birds perched next to one another on one arc. I was ready with a, "Spill it, bird,", but Hillary beat me to it, sending me a shut-up-let-me-handle-this look. "Miss Kiki, I'm sure Jakup filled you in on our...our mission," she said, adding a question mark onto the last syllable.

"Yeah, I shared the highlights – Doug's wanting to become reliably visible so he can marry his ladylove, Hillary's wanting Lief out of her life, and the two of us wanting to find the Mark of Camael so we can save the world, bring peace among all beings— and stay alive while finishing the job."

Plus get paid plenty for risking our lives, I added silently.

"Yeah, all that," I said aloud. What more could I add after that glory hound hogged the limelight? I gritted my teeth and tried to make nice. "So where do we have to go to dig up this Mark tablet thing—assuming we need to dig at all."

"We got you covered," Kiki and Jakup commented in unison.

Jakup leaned forward and began scratching in the dirt. I bent down to see what he had sketched. Since when did he get artistic—after all he couldn't sing or dance— but the outline he'd drawn was, without doubt, the Island of Hawaii. He added a squiggle here, a line there, and an arrow, then shoved up some grit and rocks into a mound.

Kiki eyed his map. "Not bad, Scrub Jay. You've shown where we are now, but, in all fairness, what I think the two humans and whatever-that-guy-is want to know is where they need to go. Do you remember my directions?"

"Does a mouse eat grain? Does a fish swim? Does a bear...?" Jakup asked.

"We get your point. You're di Vinci incarnated. I warn you—I better not have been wearing poop for nothing," I said, addressing Kiki and getting testy.

"Poop is the final resort I use when everything else has failed. Every attempt I made to contact you in another way went nowhere. Everything I tried—zippo. You must be color blind and tone deaf."

"When...?" I started.

"Never mind, Riley. She's here now, and she and Jakup have reached an agreement," Hillary said in a tone so like Mom's I spun to make sure Mom hadn't snuck up on us.

"Wait a bloody second, what agreement? I asked. "What did you agree to, Bird?"

"Chill, Partner. Let's you and I talk about this later. Everything is copacetic, but the whole world doesn't need to know," Jakup said.

I wasn't happy, but I went along. No one was going to accuse me of being the one to queer the deal. "So I see the island, the question is where on the island?"

The surface of the dirt in Jakup's drawing began to move and lumps appeared – valleys and mountains I guessed, then a saucer-like thing. Stuff started to spew out of the crater.

"The Caldera of Kilauea, of course," Kiki the pueo said.

"Shit, man. You expect us to go in the caldera? You've gotta be kidding. The USGS reported a huge explosion yesterday. We'd be nothing but toast down there," Doug said.

Wow, he must be like majorly upset. I've never heard him swear before.

I took advantage of the general shock and moved closer to Hillary. "Just how effective is that stuff, Hillary-?"

This was not looking good for the home team.

♦ ♦ ♦

CHAPTER THIRTY-EIGHT

"No way, Jose. That is a friggin' crazy idea. Kilauea's caldera is four hundred feet down and the Halema`uma`u pit is deeper yet. We're talking two miles across—that's around six square miles, guys," I said. "What was your ancestor thinking, Doug? He musta had at least one loose screw to think this was the thing to do. What in the world possessed him to come up with this boner of an idea for a hidey hole?"

Doug sagged, sad written all over his body. We strained to hear his dull, "I don't know. This is impossible." He paused for a few seconds, then we heard, "Crikey, what do we do now? By all the gods, Darcy...Darcy," he wailed.

The rest of us fell into an awkward silence at his performance. Hillary opted to speak up to try to distract him.

"I think I do," said Hillary in a hushed voice. "The legends points to where we should seek the Mark of Camael. Not far from where we are now is the site which, besides being said to be the home of Pele, is where the epicenter of a powerful psychic vortex lies, one of the most potent on earth. Can't you sense the forces circulating here?"

"We're sitting in the middle of earthquake central?" I asked. "Sorry, I like my ground solid and shake-free. The last time I was in a quake, I lost my commemorative Giants Coke bottle."

"By the gods, I don't get where you're coming from. You're supposed to be on a pure intentions quest to bring about world peace and you're still stewing over some bottle. This epicenter is not *that* kind of epicenter. Don't you understand how anything works? What do they teach you humans anyway?" Not finished, Kiki continued with, "No doubt your partner has learned the ins and outs of multiple universes."

Jakup, of course, bobbed his head and puffed up his feathers. "What I didn't pick up in flock instruction, I mastered working for the Witches Local as a free-lance familiar. You can't be a success in that profession without some solid supernatural background."

"Bull-pucky. What you learned is how to lay donkey dung on thick," I mindsent him.

He turned his back to me and told the others, "I'll fill him in."

I was so tired of the two birds getting their jollies double-teaming me. The attitude of this shit-spurting owl was getting old. I snapped. "Yeah, then what kind of epicenter?"

Hillary put her hand on my arm. "Calm down, Riley. I doubt many have heard of vortexes, far less understand them. A vortex is a place where the natural and supernatural worlds —some say spiritual—draw close, and, at times, they meld. A vortex is a window into space and time, a place where our universe co-exists with others. I imagine this would have seemed an ideal hiding place to Doug's ancestor."

"Hmm," I said glancing around, "Looks like every other pile of lava to me. Red, rough, and hot as hell in the sun."

"Maybe if you'd open—you know, the same way as when you are getting ready to `port?" she suggested.

Just for grins, I humored her and slipped into a light trance. Nothing for a second or two and then ... hot dog, the place did seem different. The colors were brighter, the shadows more ...shadowy. I could swear I heard a U2 song far off, faint. Maybe there was something to this vortex thing. The wind grew stronger and I smelled strands of good and evil. In my peripheral vision, I grew aware of figures moving along the rim, misshapen figures, large figures, teeny-tiny creatures tagging behind. Not my idea of a good time. I broke my trance.

"Okay, I'll buy some of the vortex hype. I sense something way different here— and not all of it seems right to me."

"I understand. I can't experience this as much as you do. You have spent more time with the supernatural, but even with my limited exposure to things not mundane, I'm uncomfortable, edgy-like, you know. Did you...how...how long did you think you got in touch with what was around you?" she asked.

"A long time, hours," I said.

"No more than a minute or two, Buddy," said Doug.

"I wondered because people say this vortex, besides being so strong, causes a crack in time on occasion," Hillary said.

"So we might be able to intercept my ancestor and get the mark direct from him?" Doug said, excitement oozing out his pores.

"No human, or whatever you are, can change events of the past," Kiki said in disapproval.

For the second time, I almost felt sorry for Doug, a new record. Officious jerk or not, no one likes to see a grown guy sobbing his heart out. I'd about decided to go over to give him a comforting man hug, but Hillary beat me there, holding him tight, letting his head rest on her shoulder. Great. This wasn't fair—I didn't need any more obstacles messing up my play for Hillary.. His whole body seemed in spasm from the drawn-out gasps of his weeping.

I couldn't help myself, "But we might get lucky and see your ancestor placing the table. We'd know where to look."

He nodded, still dejected. "I suppose."

CHAPTER THIRTY-NINE

Everyone stood around. No one moved. All together, they looked like a passable impression of the Tikis we'd seen earlier.

"Sorry, man, but if we're going to do what we need to do to give you a shot at Darcy, the time for action is now. We need to tighten up our game, work on the criteria. Figure out what we might face and how we could deal with things like – say 145 degrees Fahrenheit, that's about 63 degrees Celsius for you lab types," I said to distract them and thanking my physics 101 Prof, Johann Silcox, who'd drummed converting one system to the other into my weary brain. He never missed an opportunity to rail about how this country needed to join the rest of the world and use metric so young people in the states didn't need to learn yet another redundant system. I agreed with him –having to make conversions all the time sucked.

Doug's head shot up and his shoulders stiffened. "You're right, Riley. I just lost it for a second. Just thinking about life without Darcy...." He got half a sob out and drew in a deep breath.

Kiki's flutelike voice broke in. "About time you humans start to get your act together. After I go out of my way to help you. You are damn lucky there's an intelligent avian in your crew or you'd be totally clueless—and you have a brass set to call yourself a detective, "she said, staring right at me. Owl stares with those two big eyes are intimidating...and effective.

Jakup preened and stopped just short of prancing. "I try," he said in false modest tones, "but you sell Riley short. We've been partners for a long time now, and he's shown some skill with psychic phenomena."

Jakup saying nice things about me? What's next? A solar eclipse?

"Good thing. You'll need to draw on everything he's got. With luck, that's all you'll need, but my guess would be every one of you'll need to give a hundred and ten per cent or chalk this quest up to a learning experience," she said, adding what I suspected was the owl version of a doubting sniff.

"I've read some about the volcanos in Hawaii," Hillary said. "They've fascinated me since I arrived here. I went on the Crater Rim drive several times with a friend. I was surprised when I first learned the base didn't seem to be completely filled with hot lava."

"You're sort of right. Most of the live lava is *makai*," Kiki agreed.

I shot Hillary a questioning glance. She mouthed "in the direction of the sea" back to me.

Kiki was still talking. "The message I am called to present to you is: "Those who seek with good intent shall dwell without fear in the house of Pele.'"

I groaned, "Not another freakin' riddle."

"Maybe not," said Hillary. "I believe there is a legend of Pele and some other god living in the Halema`uma`u Crater. A kind of Hawaiian version of Romeo and Juliette, I think."

I noticed Jakup stiffened and assumed his commune with Betty-at-OWIS-stance and asked, "So what's the deal, Partner?"

"According to Betty, Hillary's guess is close, but in this case, they marry but their basic nature means they are fated to fail. She says despite their intense love for each other, their basic natures did not allow them to share their lives. Too different. He was the spirit of plants and greenery, while she was fire. Flames destroy greens, don't you know. Sort of like the positive end of two magnets repel each other, if you get what I mean."

"I remember now," Hillary said. "This clash explains the curse of Pele."

"You mean that crap about anyone taking the children of Pele—meaning the rocks in Halema1`uma`u—will endure bad luck until they return the stones. I read somewhere that the hotels are forever getting packets of rocks and sand from former tourists trying to shed the curse."

"Yes," said Kiki, "Pele can be a vengeful goddess, which is why anyone seeking something in the crater must have the most benevolent of intentions. Anything less ...."

I ran my finger over my throat.

"Which we do," said Doug. "Peace and love in the world and all that."

"Would a guy trying to get it on with his girl-friend meet the standard?" I asked.

Kiki perched unmoving for a moment, her head turned the one eighty toward me. Owls totally freak me out when they do that. "I believe Doug's motives would be— yours maybe not. Pele does not do selfish."

Doug jumped up, all excited. "That's why," he shouted, "that's why my ancestor hid the tablet in the crater. He wasn't so dumb, after all. Evildoers would face instant retribution—the fiery kind— while those of us seeking love would be safe from her wrath."

Jakup's head bobbed, "Makes sense. Safer, anyway."

Too much of a coincidence for me. This seemed too easy. Too many dominos falling the same direction. Too many snake eyes thrown in a row at the craps table. Coincidences are hardly ever the real solution to a problem. "How big is the area we need to concentrate on? "I asked.

Jakup did his phony academic tone again. "About a mile wide circle— one hundred thirty or so meters for you, Doug—and three hundred or so down. The good news for you bi-peds is the lava has receded from most of the pit. Of course, volcanos being volcanos, at any time a new vent could open and throw out more molten rock or a fault give way and enlarge the caldera."

I groaned. "Oh, joy, so all we need to do—providing Pele doesn't get testy—is to go down a steep cliff, cover a huge surface bit by bit, avoid getting cooked, and hope what we are looking for is in the no-molten lava part. Peachy."

The others didn't seem all that worried.

I was.

CHAPTER FORTY

Hillary spent the next hour loading the sack on my back with so much crap I'd pass for a camp-llama—either that or I was doing one of the best camel imitations of all time, the one-humped variety. To be fair, Hillary and Doug toted comparable bundles. We'd spent last night writing lists of everything we could think of we might need – stuff like oxygen bottles, climbing tools, lots of water, heavy fire resistant coveralls. The Big Box lunches were number one on my list. Doug insisted on packing full climbing gear, even after I asked why when I'd be 'porting us all. My suggestion that I stay at the top while they took turns searching for the Mark fell flat.

I tried, "If I 'port you one after another, you'd get a break. Scanning is tedious"

"Not a chance, Riley. Either we're all in or you give it a go on your own. Remember I'm the one paying you the big bucks," said Doug.

Put that way, I was on board for the trip.

I'd argued why we needed to schlep all this when I could 'port whatever we needed whenever we needed it. Jakup's answer was a scrub jay stink eye in spades, "Are you planning to 'port out, pack into wherever for whatever you need, and then 'port back in time for us so we'd not turn into an overdone roast or an organic cinder? If so, you can count the rest of us out."

My sulk was short. He indeed had a point. I'd spent most of the day yesterday locating and retrieving the items on the list Hillary and Doug put together. I'd added on my few things—Tex-Mex trail mix, extra lunches, and a spare pair of fireproof boots. The rest of my page duplicated the items on their epic length shopping lists.

Next step was our pre-flight check. First, we did the last minute once-over of our paraphernalia, "Water bottles?"

"Six each, check."

"Ropes?"

"Check."

"Those weird gloves with the hard stuff on the palms?"

"Check, three."

"Okay, that's it. Everyone ready for a visit to Volcanos National Park? Get in close and intertwine hands. Jakup, you got my usual pocket?"

"Nesting comfortably, Partner," he replied.

"Okay, let's go."

"Wait," said Hillary. "I'm going back for a batch of the protection power and the barrier blend, just in case."

"Good call, Hil," I said. When she came back carrying one glass and one plastic container, I shot her a questioning glance.

"The barrier stuff needs to be in an impervious container," she answered.

"Okay, now are we ready?"

After a chorus of uh huhs, I got the show on the road. I went through my final mental pre-flight. Slowed my breathing and cleared my mind. Lastly, I did something Hillary called emptying my chakras—whatever they were. "Cleared for take-off," I said.

I caught the dumbfounded expression on the face of a customer near the parking lot railing as our small clump of humankind disappeared, One of the best ever. I aimed for the museum close by the Observatory. We'd talked back and forth, about where would be the best and closest site near our destination. I was sure the Observatory would still be there, volcano or no volcano.

I figured if something big had happened and mounds of molten rock reached that far, the local TV would have been covering the story twenty-four seven. I didn't want to take a chance on dropping down directly into the crater. Landing on some new lava'd make us old news. We emerged onto the overlook. No screams should be a good omen for our mission.

Peering down gave me a tight throat and a gulp. The haze and faint reddish glow signaled this would be no picnic. The wind picked up and delivered a pot-load of rotten egg aroma. Kudos to Doug for including gas masks on his list. Our self-proclaimed expert told us,

"Hydrogen sulfide can cause throat and lung irritation, even cause an asthma attack...or death. We always had to turn on the ventilation fans and wear masks when we worked with the stuff. What we're about to do— heavy physical exertion walking and climbing around— would exacerbate the effects., he proclaimed.

I was down with his reasoning. Couldn't hurt and maybe the stink'd be less. Made me want to puke.

I adjusted the hat I'd decided to wear— more Doug advice— and was glad I had when I heard the telltale plop of poop. I looked up, and, there she was, wings flapping, the world-class shitbird herself.

"I wanted to catch you before you went down. Remember the line about entering the caldera only if you have pure intent? I decided you deserved a warning, Riley. The others should be good to go, but how pure have your efforts in this enterprise been? Pele doesn't mess around. Goddesses don't take kindly to poseurs."

"What's a poseur?"

"A phony with devious plans and a questionable goal."

"Oh."

Three heads turned my way. I swallowed hard.
Was I? Did I?
Yikes.

CHAPTER FORTY-ONE

Did I? Was I? Did I? Was I? I swallowed deep. All eyes were on me.

"Well, do you?" demanded Doug. "Have a pure heart, I mean? No self-serving goals and no ulterior motives? I sure as hell hope so because...because we're ...like depending on you, you know."

I did know. I, more than any of them, realized the others couldn't go on their own—except Jakup, maybe. Even then, if the tablet was too heavy, he might not be able to retrieve and carry the thing long enough to stay away from the fumes and heat of the caldera. I glanced over at Kiki for a second or two—she'd stuck around to watch how we did, more likely to gloat if we tanked. This was enough to tell me she was not only a no. she was a hell no. If I tried to 'port 'em down into the crater, and I flunked the altruism test, we'd fail. Never mind our fee. Doug didn't get his girl, Hillary would have to deal with Lief on her own, and the war gods would be free to set up their war games, maybe even stage a volcanic fry-party.

"Partner?" asked Jakup, with an anxious tone in his voice. "You okay, you can handle this, right?"

I wanted so much to say yes, just yes and let's get on with it, but my throat froze and the words wouldn't come out. I sunk down and put my face between my palms. The deep trance state I used to 'port fell over me uninvited, and I commenced an internal debate with myself. Being a drama king and acting, this way was so not me.

"Am I pure in heart? Are my goals for the benefit of others? Done with no thought for myself? What does pure in heart and good intentions mean anyway?" I asked my inner self.

"Don't you member anything from that philosophy class you took? Pure in heart means not hypocrisy, not bull-shitting, not hidden motives."

"He never said bull-shitting," I said.

"Well, that's what he meant. Are you doing this for the money or would you be satisfied with solving Doug and Hillary's problems and not making a dime?"

"I'd never considered either one." '

"You need to be honest with yourself. No going around and more tooting your horn and patting yourself on the back. You'd be kicked off the team before you start."

My inner self pulled no punches. Either I was or I wasn't. No politician's posturing or excuses for me. If I said what I did came from a good place, but then I didn't clear the bar set by the Mark, we might all end up par-broiled. No second chances.

"Well, yes, but what about the saving the world thing? Doesn't that count? Don't I get an automatic pass for taking on the quest? Doing what's necessary to achieve success?"

"Not unless you can honestly say the good of all was your goal from the beginning—not influenced by the prospect of an on-going relationship with Hillary or getting a flashy fast boat for you to use as a chick-magnet on the Bay."

What kind of entity would be such a hardass? I sank further down in my trance, deeper than I could remember having plunged before. I'd never probed into myself so intensely. Never questioned why I did things or treated people.

"Come on—I'm new at this. Like for a long time, years, I didn't even realize I had psychic abilities when I got into this game. Some of the stuff I did when I was pledge master in the frat was only for fun and games—no harm, no foul— and I became good buds with the plebes afterward. I didn't want to hurt them."

"Or take the time that I dipped the neighbor cat's tail in red paint. After a while, the hair grew back and her tail was back to normal again. How could whatever or whoever created the tablet hold my past actions against me? If my interior motives were unconscious, I should get a pass." I sniveled.

"Should you? My inner self answered.

An icey fear filled me. I shivered. *"Was saving the world from a nuclear holocaust and fighting the good fight against a hoard of malevolent devils really accomplish our goals?"*

I didn't get around to answering because my partner was using his beak and all his talons to rouse me.

"You okay, Partner? Snap out of it. We got work to do. A world to save."

I shot up from my trance, stood up, and said, "I guess, but let me go along first, just to make sure—so none of you are toast."

Hillary came over and gave me a huge hug, "We'll go together, Riley. You just proved you are ethical and acting for the good of all."

Hope to hell, she's right or we're all goners. One large bead of sweat slid down my forehead.

CHAPTER FORTY-TWO

"Hey, you over there—yeah, you," he said as I pointed at my chest.

"You all will have to move," the red-haired guy in the ranger's uniform yelled, waving at us and heading our way. "Move back, away from the edge—way back behind the fence."

"He's calling a strand or two of wimpy wire a fence? Get real, Dude."

"Now," he added in an emphatic tone.

This idiot shows up when we were precisely two nano-seconds away from my 'port ETA. His hollering and the clumping of his heavy ranger issue boots had broken my concentration. I'd never get us off heading where we needed to be. I turned his way and demanded, "Why?" And this better be good."

The dude was rude, and, besides, we didn't need delays.

"First of all, because I told you to, and secondly, if we had an earthquake, standing on the rim would be unwise—unless you enjoy being mashed and fried," he said, puffing from his short run to reach the spot where we stood —on the opposite side of the fence, on the parking lot side. Talk about being out of shape, this clown was super soft and in major need of the 10-minute conditioning program. He panted at irregular intervals—pant, pant, gasp, silence, silence, pant—like he needed to remember to breathe.

"Now," he ordered.

"What's up his butt? He doesn't have to be such a jerk," I mindsent Jakup. *"Aren't Park Rangers supposed to be courteous and kind?"*

"You're thinking of Boy Scouts. We might as well move back. Your mind's in no shape to 'port anyone now."

I shrugged, just as Hillary said, blinking her eyes. "We're so sorry, Sir. We weren't aware. We didn't see any sign telling us to stay behind the fence."

He shot us another of his way-over-the-top expressions, "Well, naughty us. We assumed most people would realize we put up a railing to keep folks on one side for a reason. Apparently, you mainlander-haoles are a bit slow so I assume you do things differently stateside."

"Now wait a minute." Doug began.

I could tell, from the edge in his voice, he was pissed. I'd been wrong about him. He did have human-type emotions, and, right now, dissed as a dummy, he was hot. Having their intellect questioned, like, mega-bothers science types. Some of the physics majors got downright rude if you pointed out an error on their lab report. I found that out the hard way my freshman year.

Didn't take a rocket scientist to guess the way this dude was acting hadn't sat well with Doug. Fuming came to mind. He had both his hands clenched, and I noticed he'd begun to grind his jaw. He'd been wholly visible when this started, but now he was fading.

"Hold it, man," I said to him. "I know how you feel, but let's get on the other side of this sorry excuse for a fence and carry on there. Wait until you get yourself back into the spectrum before unloading on him."

He glanced down at the spot where his arm should be, shot me a sideways glance, and muttered, "Why does this always happen to me?"

"Why? Because what you want least always shows up at the worst possible time," I said. "Melvin's law."

"Murphy's," he corrected and grimaced as he shuffled toward the fence.

The two birds in our band took off and headed in tandem for the closest perching spot. Happy to see Kiki had done her thing on the ranger, I smiled my most evil smile as he sputtered, wiping the stuff off his forehead and cheeks. I had one of those pretend napkins, the kind they have in fast food places, which are about four by six and one ply. "Would this help?" I asked the ranger in a phony helpful voice.

His only thanks were a dirty look my way. "Okay, the rest of you move your butts behind the railing."

"He's not a real ranger, Riley," Hillary mouthed my way. "No park employee would talk this way to the public."

"You're right, Hil," I whispered back. She was right, but for the wrong reason. Rude by itself didn't cut the mustard. Rude plus a rapidly growing line of fresh greenery and bushes growing up through the asphalt did. The out of place plants partly masked a gaggle of shifters. Now we had clear confirmation. No more than thirty seconds passed before he gestured them to head our way.

Hoo boy. Trouble, we got trouble, bad stuff be brewin' on the Big Island.

Bigger tufts of grass and shrubs grew up as they advanced from the far side of the lot in what the National Guard guys would call a flanking movement. The green ferns signaled Kamapua`a, was on the scene, although his porcine shape faded in an out with a human form to make him less obvious. The super-buffed mega-male figure of Ku led one group while some Greekish guy led the others--all armed with war clubs. I spotted Lief and our scaled covered waiter behind him. To say we were out-numbered and ill-equipped to make a stand was an understatement.

"Riley, we need to regroup and leave this place. The ranger has red hair and Pele's ex is the god of plants and vegetation. I think the gods are making a move on us," Hillary said.

"Duh."

"I agree, but why now? We don't have the Mark yet and the crater is a huge hostile place. Their timing is way off," Doug said.

She nodded and I shot her a "Couldn't agree more" as I grabbed her hand, put my other hand of Doug's shoulder. "*Pocket now, Partner!* I mindsent, and a blue and white streak headed my way. Kiki followed. I remember thinking, "Now where the hell do I have a place to put an owl that big," as I `ported us to what I hoped would be a safe site.

CHAPTER FORTY-THREE

Dropping directly from the real world into Between drained me like frat guy downs a cold brewski on a hot day. Whipped, I sank back not quite sure where I'd put down. Most likely, the last place sitting on top of my cortex or medulla whichever one of those would keep such things. Wadya know—we landed back at Penelope's. My primeval need for food moved to its safe zone.

"As long as we're here, we might as well order something," I suggested.

"Do you ever have anything besides food on your mind?" Doug asked.

"Apparently not," I said, not giving a sh...whit.

Hillary surveyed the near-by tables checking if anyone noticed the sudden appearance of three people and two birds. The booths had high backs, so not. "This might be the perfect spot to tackle the caldera. All the excitement gave me an appetite, too."

Now she was coming round to my way of doing things. Maybe there's hope for me with this nifty chick yet.

Although we should be safe in the closed in booth, as a precaution, I set about to creating a layer of fuzziness around us. Anyone looking in wouldn't see much. Obscuring was so much easier than an opaque bubble. With my energy level so low, I doubted I could come up with a credible shield anyway.

"Considering our near miss, we have work to do. I, for one, don't have a clue why the gods decided to make a move on us at the overlook. Doesn't make sense. Why would they? We're almost as far in the dark about where Doug's great, great something stashed the Mark as they are. Now whatever tiny tidbits of knowledge we gleaned from owl friend may be theirs as well—not directly, but inferred. They've leaned where we intend to search."

"Cutting things pretty close this time, didn't you, Partner," Jakup said. His head bobbed up and down as he viewed everyone sitting to his left and his right. Those darn offset eyes give him an unfair advantage in a crowd. "Where we planned to search is neither here nor there. We've got to figure out how they learned we'd be at the caldera. Did one of us let something slip around the wrong person?"

We all shook our collective heads, except Kiki.

We stared at her as her head did a one eight oh turn. "Hey, don't look at me," she said. "I'm on the side of the good guys. Nobody wins if those dickheads get another war started. Personally, I'm not found of more good nesting ground shot hell by idiots trampling all over the place, not to say pelting good trees with flying objects besides. Clumsy buggers."

Wow, tough language coming from an owl.

Jakup ignored her. "Then, we need to come up with a way to be stealthy, more surreptitious as Sherlock would say. If we aren't careful what we say or what we do, we're screwed," he said. "Any ideas how the rest of you plan to fly-over the search area without getting spotted? Natural aviators such as Kiki and I have had generations to perfect the flit and fade, but ...."

"We don't," Doug finished for him. Every part of his semi-visible body seemed to sag.

"I'm too new at this witch stuff to be as effective at tasks as I need to be, I'm afraid," Hillary said. "Spells and potions, yes. Invisible night flights, no."

All eyes turned to me. I felt like the guy sitting in the witness chair as an obnoxious prosecutor chucked hostile questions at him. "Where were you between the hours of 7 and 10:30 on the night of September 7, 2001?"

How the hell would I know?

What I did know was I was the key player on this team—no one else had a magic skeleton key, no one else had the entry code to the way in. Riley Rose, superhero? Sure, I've proven I'm a top notch psychic, a natural in interspecies communication, able to teleport in this dimension and points Between, but in that precise moment, I'd never felt so overwhelmed. I finally understood what we were up against – an alliance of powerful war gods. Any one of them was many times worse than the Wereweasel I bested, more evil than the bevy of sap-sucking Vampires, none of them was a one and done evil creature. We faced an army of angry bad news supernaturals determined to regain all their past power and then some. What stood in their way to block their progress toward in their goals?

Just me. Riley Rose. Scared shitless psychic.

I glanced down at my feet, unzipped a pocket in my backpack, and rummaged around until I found a packet of trail mix. My stomach was in knots. I found a packet, popped the wrapper, and chewed. I couldn't wait for the omelet I ordered. For the first time ever food didn't help. I had no choice. Even though I was one urp away from a barf, I sat up straight and assumed the pose of a leader. "I can fly us. I can create an obscuring bubble. I might be even be able to set up protective shield against the heat but no guarantees. I sure as hell can't do all three at once."

"Betty told me molten lava get up to over two thousand degree Fahrenheit – twelve hundred degrees Celsius. We'd need to block at least that much. Think you could swing that?" Jakup asked.

The expression on my face was his answer. "No, make that hell, no," I said.

Two glum faces and two sets of unblinking bird eyes said what we all were thinking. We're royally fu...forked.

"I've got an idea," said Doug. "I remember when we had a chem-fire in the lab. The firemen wore this kind of space-suit gear, lots of breathing tubes and oxygen. If we got some of those, we'd take care of the heat problem—mostly anyway."

"Great idea, Doug," Hillary said, "but where would we get hold suits like that?"

Jakup's head had already assumed his on-line. "Okay, Betty, I'm sorry, too. Most fire departments buy their firefighting equipment on the net. Betty says no suppliers are located in Hawaii—all on the mainland, mostly on the east coast."

"We can't borrow some from the closest fire station. They might stuff like that for an emergency," I said. "I wonder if there is a second hand store handling them."

"No," said Jakup, "but the Hawaii Community College has a firefighting department. We might score what we need there."

"We'd only need three," said Doug, "Jakup and Kiki should be able to fit in one of our helmets."

The two birds glanced at one another and I swear they did something physically impossible. They shrugged.

"Let's move," said Jakup.

I plied my fork double time and gobbled my food. I told myself I'd need all the energy I could get.

I pulled out my phone and did a quick Google search for the college. I sucked in a deep breath and `ported us off to scrounge up some snazzy fire suits. Revised Step 1 in our Retrieve Mark itinerary. Many more revisions and we might have to bag the whole thing.

CHAPTER FORTY-FOUR:

Step one: college campus. Check.

Safely back in real space in front of the admin building, I gestured toward a bench-high wall, "Wait here, I'll be right back," I said and opened the door to the office.

"Hi, there," I said smiling and sending the girl behind the counter a strong psychic suggestion—one I wouldn't take a no for an answer. "Take us to the part of the college where they teach firefighting."

"I can't. I'm on duty until twelve. Why anyway?' she tried to ask before the suggestion took hold big time. Blank-faced, she headed down a hallway, out the door and hung a right for the direction we needed to go. A short walk later, she stopped and pointed.

"Close but no cigar,

" I said, "I want the storage area for their equipment."

"I don't have authorization to go in there," she answered.

"Point us to the right door, and I'll handle that part."

I could tell she didn't want to, but my suggestion to get a move on was persuasive. She led us around a building to the back and down to the door marked "Fire Fighting Equipment."

"Okay, thanks. You can go back to work now—oh, you can forget you ever saw us here," I added.

She left without a word. In another time and another place, I'd go with her. She was at least an eight, my usual type to work at knowing better.

"Let's see if there's a changing room in this store."

The next hour we played dress up. Try on a suit, too big, too small, wrong color. Pick out a helmet. We paused in the fashion show to read through the instructions for the breathing apparatus. Knowing how to use the paraphernalia struck me as a good idea at the time.

"These things are a lot more complicated than the ones we had in the lab," Doug complained.

"What we got is what we got," Hillary said.

"As long as we don't test the upper limits of the suits too long," Doug said, "We'll probably be okay."

Probably?

At five minutes past four, we all had suits, helmets, gloves, breathing equipment, belts, and boots. Hillary looked ready for a part in a circus—her footwear was way big on her feet, but perfect for a clown act.

"If I stuff a sock in each toe and keep my other shoes on inside the boots, I think I'm good to go," she said.

"Sunset is in a couple hours, if my calculations are correct," Doug said. "More than enough time to stop in Hilo for a shave ice and some taro fries."

He went up three notches in my what-kind-of-a-guy-is-he scale. I didn't hesitate and set us down on the main drag, mere feet away from the closest stand. I snagged some peanuts for Jakup. Kiki said she wasn't hungry. "I had a good hunt this morning—scored a plump mouse."

We all sat on a bench, eating and watching the sky turn pink. A full-on sunset would have been better, but the pink, peach, and oranges above us with purple cloud blotches weren't all that bad either. Hillary used the time to scan the book Mom'd given her to search for some quick and easy mists to mask us on our tour over the caldera. Doug and I were both quiet, lost in thought. Everyone sat intimidated by the task in front of us.

"I read the vortex over the caldera is powerful, much more than most," said Doug, breaking the silence.

"I wouldn't think you science guys would buy into stuff like vortexes," I said.

"Maybe the average lab rat wouldn't, but I'm not average, remember? Being not-quite-human is why I'm on this expedition. I'm hoping this doesn't turn out to be a wild goose chase."

He turned his back on me suddenly, and I realized tears were crawling down his cheeks. Maybe my original estimation of him was way off —the nerd liked food, loved his girl, and carried some interesting, if normally useless, bits of information around in his head, ready for easy access. The girl love part was welcome because this meant he wouldn't be on the make for Hillary, which left the field wide open for me.

I turned to give him some privacy and noticed Jakup and Kiki were beak to beak in some heavy conversation. To break the tension, I asked Jakup, "What's up, Partner? You and Kiki got the world's problems solved?"

Kiki answered with a dismissive chirp, "No, unlike humans, we avians tend to business and don't get distracted by trivialities. Putting my background knowledge together with the data your partner got from OWIS, we have come up with a strategy for our overflight of the caldera."

I glanced at Jakup, and he nodded.

Kiki then went on a long-winded diatribe about access point to the vortex, crack in the symbiotic structure, chains of dancing blue fire, leeching the ley line. I understood about nothing. Her explanation was worse than Doug's speaking total scientist jargon. I wasn't even going to try. I was more worried about how I was going to maneuver all of us above the floor of the crater to search without going Between. We needed to stay in our dimension for this hunt.

"So where do we need to go first?" I asked mimicking every taxi driver I'd ever ridden with.

"Back to the observatory, Partner."

"You got it." I said, trying to put as much confidence into my voice as I could. I didn't want to bring up a thought that suddenly occurred to me. *"How would we recognize the Mark? We didn't know what the thing looked like."*

CHAPTER FORTY-FIVE

Considering what Kiki told us about the crack in the vortex—and assuming the fracture did exist—we'd decided we should try to take as much advantage of the fissure as possible. First, though, we needed to conduct a grid-by-grid search of the caldera floor to locate where the fracture intersected with the rim. I sensed another attempt at sidetracking and tried to argue. "Do we really want to pursue that cracked vortex thing? So far, our efforts amount to nothing except delays, detours, and downright dodgy screw-ups. Why don't we focus on the how instead of searching for where to start?"

"Doesn't your partner have a brain?" Kiki asked Jakup.

"Most of the time," he said. "Why?"

"Because, throwing away the one small advantage these ill-equipped participants possess seems ill-advised to me," she said, succeeding in coating each word with owlish scorn.

Heads bounced north and south, and I was out-voted.

"Okay then. Hand me the trail mix," I said. If I had to go on a psychic pre-search, I needed nourishment. I would like some small part of my life to stay in a waking rather than trance state. How's a guy supposed to have a life, obsessing on his chakras? I'm sure of one thing. I'm done with all this heavy supernatural stuff. Jakup and I will need to agree to put the fairy tale folks back in the book and not in my life. We can get plenty of cases where we use my psychic abilities in our own universe.

"*Better tend to business, Rose. That was then, this is now,*" Jakup mindsent.

He was eavesdropping on my thoughts.

Put that way, I wanted to respond, "Must you always be this snarky?" but aloud I answered. "Okay, you might have a point. I'll go along. "

I zoned and zeroed in on the outlines of the vortex. I followed a line—a glowing one, like the lights in the aisles in an airplane they claim should show you how to reach the exits in a crash situation—leading into the surrounding twists. I'd never tell anyone when this was over, but this scared me shitless. I sensed the writhing bands of energy housed in the vortex and I freaked. Hot one minute, cold the next, shivering, panting ... however many body reactions were possible – I got them all and at the same time.

From somewhere I heard, "You don't belong here."

I got the message and moved out, following the dragon tail of the turbulence. I made a vow never to complain again, when the pilot came on the loudspeaker saying, "We may be experiencing some mild turbulence."

I curved up and down, turned left, turned right. *There has to be a better way.*

I'd no sooner thought this when I spotted my quarry or target, to be exact. On the side of the rim, not quite to the top of the caldera, was a too-black slice in the rock. When I got close, I was able to see the sides undulating in unison with the center of the vortex. *If this ain't it, I'll put in with you.* '

To hell with the turns and twists, I shot up pdq and beat it back to the spot where the others waited. Time would tell how well we'd fare in our solid form instead of my psychic projection.

I reeled and fell on my butt when I arrived at the observatory where the others waited.

"What's wrong, Riley? Are you hurt? Were you attacked?" Hillary asked.

"*You okay, Partner?*" Jakup mindsent.

Being the center of your own universe is no fun. I waited until the world around me stopped whirling, only then could I manage an "Uh huh."

"Did you find it, the vortex crack, I mean?" asked Doug. Not hard to tell where his priorities were. Like back on the mainland in a lab.

"Yeah—I followed the lay line running through the what-ever-you-call an invisible whirlpool. On the side of the rim," I said pointing to a hazy black line. "I think we ought to rethink going to the bottom that way. You saw how I was when I got here. I don't know if I can keep our bodies all in one piece going down."

The crack swayed back and forth and, every once in a while, veered in the opposite direction. Even though I traveled out-of-body, I had all I could do going down the chute not to toss my trail mix.

"Figures," said the snarky flute noise I'd grown to hate. "Proves humans don't have their shit together enough to complete a job. Go home, then—or why did you come in the first place?"

Put that way, I turned to my cohorts and asked, "Ready to go?"

CHAPTER FORTY-SIX

"Just so you are clear about what we might face—this is my plan. I approach the break in the rim from the top, then slam down toot sweet into the opening and then make like an elevator going down on a broken cable until we hit the same plane as the floor of the pit."

"Did you test this plan?" Mr.-Scientific-Hypothesis-guy, Doug, asked. "Would drop speed be the same as gravity or would other laws apply?"

"Not sure, I went bodiless, remember?" I said, trying to sound more confident than I felt. "I figure going in a group and me going alone wouldn't be comparable. If I went ahead and tried a normal body run I'd learn less—plus, if I ended up on a one way and didn't make a round trip, what would I have proven? Less than nothing. On the other hand, if we all go together, and don't complete a round trip, we'd all be goners and would care less. We might as well go for broke. And, yes, if you want to know," I said staring straight at Kiki, "yes, I am scared shitless."

"If we fail, what are our chances of surviving and finding another psychic with the same abilities as Riley?" Hillary asked Jakup.

My partner didn't hesitate. '"You don't want to know. Zippo, zilch. Matching up the two of us represents some serious scrying by Witches Local 723. When we first met, I thought, "This guy? No way." He'd had no training and not a clue what he could do. I put a lot of time in bringing him up to speed. Sundown's coming. How much time can you risk taking?"'

In the next minute, everything seemed totally worth it.

"Riley, you're acting like a real leader. Doug and I were lucky to find J&R. I understand now – your acting like a total idiot is just an act. Down deep you are brave and mean well." She bent over and laid a wet one right on my lips.

My joy was short-lived. My partner sniffed and lifted one foot and then the other. "Getting deep in here, isn't it? He does okay most of the time, but getting carried away with compliments doesn't work just yet. Might go right to his head, and his head is big enough already. We need to move this along. Let's do that Zen thing and mix our chakras or whatever we're supposed to do."

"Hear, hear," Kiki crowed.

I never thought owls could crow.

"Back to my plan. When we reach bottom, Kiki and Jakup, you can conduct an aerial search under your own power," I glanced up. "If one of you stumbles onto the

Mark, call me, and I'll move you two PDQ-- along with the tablet-- back to the bottom of the split in the rock. Then I'll come back to collect the rest of you up."

"Hey, how'd I get drafted into this?" Kiki asked.

"Doug, I'll 'port you left when we descend. Hillary and I will go right. I can only levitate two at once. If I try for three, we all might end up as marshmallows. At best bronze and sticky inside, at worse, brittle, and burnt."

"Let's hope these suits are enough to keep this from happening," Hillary said, straightening one side of her front fasteners. "We look like alien beings from some other dimension," she added with a giggle. "Just call me Hillary Armstrong. One small step for man, one small step for peace, and another step for Doug."

"Hear, hear," echoed all round.

"Ready bubble of obscurity?"

"Ready," she said.

"Ready the grid map of the caldera?"

"Check," said Doug.

"Aerial observation corps ready to rise."

"Jeez, Partner, can you make it a little cheesier?"

"Do you always have such notions of grandeur? This is a volcano, not the moon," Kiki added.

"Cut him some slack. Did you forget who's waiting for us to show up back at the parking lot," Jakup said, backwinging her. "Or, that for most of the light over, a quick exit courtesy of my partner is all we got between us staying our proud bird selves and being a fricassee with few feathers?"

My respect went up. I'd forgotten the part of the plan where the two left the shelter of our fire suits and flew in the buff.

"Jakup, I'll try to envelope you both with part of the blurring bubble and slip in an open space layer to help insulate." Hillary said.

"Thanks, Hillary."

Why I'm not sure, but I turned around and faced the others, throwing up my hand for a high five—just before I took us Between en route to a hole in the ground filled with fire and brimstone.

CHAPTER FORTY-SEVEN

My internal GPS performed spot on the money. We emerged at midpoint of the fissured fracture of the rim. The blast of heat sucked so much moisture out of our bodies, and we all reached at the same time for a water bottle. After several chugs, I got up enough courage to look down. In an instant, I was one with a steak searing on the grill, and, damn, bug-eyed at the sheer drop-off. Staying Between sounded preferable to cooking over a hundreds-of-feet-deep kettle.

Our survival instincts triggered an automatic group recoil. My gut retreated so far back my colon lay plastered against my backbone. My body moved to instinct mode and tried to escape the searing blast of metal-melting heat. The incandescence of the molten areas hit both my eyes with an almost physical force. I was not alone. Hillary used her hand to shield her eyes despite wearing tropical darkness sunglasses. Only Doug appeared unfazed . He may have encountered similar displays in his girlfriend's lab. He calmly pulled a light shirt over his face to do double duty against the heat and the glare. For a nano-second or two, I actually wished I had studied what he had studied so I'da known to do the same. Jakup's beak popped out of the collar of my fire suit and a similar length of Kiki's from Hillary's from between the two check bumps. I should be so lucky!

"Partner, this has got to be one quick trip, fire suits or not. You bi-peds can sink down farther, but we'll need to do our reconnaissance at no closer than rim altitude. Say good-bye to close-in scrutiny from us. Count yourself lucky we both possess the normal exceptional avian eyesight."

"Yeah, yeah, if we were to believe you, everything birdish is exceptional. I agree— if you leave the protective suit, you need to keep enough distance. Give a holler if I need to zap you to cooler climes in a hurry. No roast owl or scrub jay needed."

"Without saying, my man," said Kiki.

"Okay then. Everyone has their assignments. Supposedly, these outfits should work for forty minutes. Let's play safe and cut the time to twenty-five. If we can't put our hands on ..."

"Doug," Hillary interrupted in an unexpected and the oddest voice ever, kinda like those the mediums in the old movies used. Her words suggested echoes from some deep cavern. "Your love for Darcy will guide you. The golden path will beckon and lead you to the ...the tz'ror mounding the opening where your ancestor placed the tablet."

"What?" both Doug and I said.

"If that's true, why am I here at all?" asked Kiki.

Hillary gave a start and glanced over at us. "What?"

"Why'd you say I should be able to detect where the Mark lies? asked Doug.

"I did? Are you sure?" she answered.

My guess was she wasn't faking. "Would we ask if you hadn't?"

Jakup chipped in with, "Good point, Partner, and another question. If the lovesick scientist has his own private guide, why bring us along? I concede you're needed for transportation, but I've got other things I could be doing."

Hillary's icy non-tone materialized again. "The members of the mission must project sufficient emanations of peace and love to waken the guide. Doug must serve as the focus of the group good-will."

Unconsciously both my arms rose and the index and middle fingers on both hands assumed the V peace sign. A scent of roses filled the air. Where in the hell did that come from? Maybe the peace and love crowd from back in the Beatles era were onto something.

"Put your arms down, Riley," Hillary said in her normal voice. "You'll drop something for sure."

"Sure, Mom," I answered in a sarcastic tone. "Whatever you say."

She shot me a withering glance, breathed deep, and leaned over the abyss. "Shall we go?"

The second I hit open space, an updraft lifted me, twisting and turning. What about me attracted crosswinds, updrafts, and downdrafts in quick succession? I had not a clue. One thing for sure, something out there did not like me. What I wouldn't have given for the rudder and flaps of even the small airplane. I needed every skill I picked up from "Teleporting for Dummies" to keep my yaw and pitch under control and do my part. Hillary hung on for dear life, and Doug came close to strangling me to avoid falling. This was shaping up to be one hairy twenty-five minutes.

"Partner, I've set up a mind-merge tendril for us to keep in touch. You can pass on what you need to do to Kiki. I'll make the connection heftier than usual so the our bond doesn't break."

We did a quick two-way test to make sure everything was working, and Kiki and Jakup took off. The scant backpressure of those lightweight bodies leaving set me rolling

"Okay, Doug, on three I'm sending you left. Hillary and I will veer right. Holler when you spot the path. Got it?"

"10-4, Captain," he said.

I held our position steady as I moved Doug on his trajectory and found my wind-juggling efforts needed to double. My inner pilot picked up a rhythm in the attacking crosswinds, and I was able to stabilize us. I oriented the relative positions of Doug and the two of us in case I needed to move us the heck-outta-here in a hurry.

"Ready, Hillary?"

"Yup," she said.

"You check left and down and I'll check right and down as we circle the perimeter to come opposite Doug. When I hit 180, we head out across. I'm afraid things might prove more exciting soon ... "

Didn't take that long. A twisting shudder went through me top to bottom trying to turn me inside out. "Hang tight, Hillary."

She hugged me tighter, and that was the nice part.

CHAPTER FORTY-EIGHT

Even though I was wearing the protective fire suit as I `ported over the crater, I was sure my body-juices were only a hair short of boiling. Despite the breathing apparatus, my throat felt parched. I couldn't decide where I was the most uncomfortable, and I never realized focusing my eyes could hurt this much. Making this trip had shaped up to be the longest twenty-five minutes of my life. Levitation only goes so fast.

Hillary and I had assumed a side-by-side freefall parachutist formation, locking our inside arms locked at the elbow to keep stable and stay together. Both our heads moved side to side as if we were watching a slow motion tennis match. I'd never seen so much hot nothing as here, or been anywhere that smelled so bad. Rotten eggs times one hundred, no, times one thousand. The spurts of hot gas and molten rock made a cool display, but I would have been happy with their images on a YouTube video.

We'd gone about a quarter of the way around when the first fireball whipped by us. "Where'd that come from?" I yelled and gripped Hillary harder.

"Ouch, don't squeeze so hard," she said. "What was that thing? None of the other flares came anywhere near this high. Oh, watch out, here comes another one."

"What the hell?" I yelled as I took evasive action to avoid another blazing globe.

"Can you rotate us in a three sixty view to see what's causing all this—maybe pinpoint where they're coming from?"

"I'll try," I replied.

Making like a pinwheel was not easy. Bursts of wind and counter wind punched us, relentless down drafts pushed hard, forcing us down toward the bottom. Those three weeks of pilot training I took one semester came in handy as I struggled to keep our orientation and altitude steady. The first few fireballs snuck up without a sound. The latest couple added a nasty shriek. If I didn't know better, I'da thought they were alive.

"Something's way wrong with this," Hillary said. "None of the other bursts of flame traveled this way."

"Did you spot anything going on that came across as wrongish to you where you are, Partner?".

"We're hearing a bunch of popping noises off in the distance, kind of in your direction, but nothing here. Why?" Jakup mindsent back.

"I swear someone is using us for target practice. This crap ain't normal."

"Riley, did you see him?"

"See who?" I answered.

"OMG—there're more—a big fat one over there, some kind of snaky person near with a big red ball of white hot—OMG OMG OMG—I see that red-haired guy from the parking lot."

Didn't take a rocket scientist. That carrot-top dude was the one Jen warned us about.

"Sheesh, Hillary, Jen told us about this guy. We're in deep kimchee now, and we haven't spotted the big ugly Hawaiian war god yet. He's gotta be around, too."

"Wait a second, Riley," Hillary said, breathing hard. "Why did we split up seeing as Doug's the one who's supposed to spot the tablet? Is he okay? Do you know? With all the stuff going on here? We need to check on him."

I sure didn't argue.

"Hold tight. I'm going Between."

"Partner, have you been monitoring Doug's progress. If these asshole gods get him, we're on a goose chase, and they've won," I mindsent Jakup.

"Kiki's handling that quadrant. Let me check."

I waited for a minute or two, then he reported in. *"Good thing you thought to check on him. He's under fire as well. Lift him the hell out ... and bring Kiki and me along while you're at it."*

"Okay, send me the coordinates."

He did better than that. He sent a quick rendering of the exact path from where he calculated Hillary and I were in relation to Doug. I dipped into Between to pick up speed and set a course for Doug, snagging the two birds on the way. Good thing. A giant fireball was zooming in on target to take him out in the next couple seconds.

Damn, the coolish air of the parking lot smelled good.

"Looks like they took the first round. We need to be stealthier on our return visit. Break out the obscuring powder and whatever else you've cooked up."

"I kept some of the Adumbrato dust in reserve, plus I have some Fetor, another mixtures I was holding back because...because the stuff is mega-disgusting. Sticky, black, stinky—reminds me of sorghum syrup," she said. "If the compound tastes as bad as it smells..."

"I could give a flying crap what I smell like. I think we need to keep our hands clean though, in case the tablet insists only on a live touch."

"Sometimes you surprise me, Partner, that almost makes sense."

CHAPTER FORTY-NINE

Hillary broke out the sack of back-up obscuring stuff.

"Luckily I doubled the recipe."

The only thing good about Hillary plastering me with the foul mess she'd concocted was she was the one doing the applying. Even then, I had all I could do not to barf on her blouse. Think dog shit mixed with rotting rat and you'd come close.

"How are we supposed to slip in without them spotting us and opening fire again? We reek so bad anything with a nose should have no trouble locating us."

"Ordinarily, you'd be right, but these fumes are meant to tighten the skin on the shell I spun around us. Bind the molecules, or some such," said Hillary. "At least that's what the directions said. And most supernaturals would find the scent pleasant anyway."

"Dandy for them, but I feel like I've been dumpster diving in a litter box."

"Oh, hush. Remember that pure of heart thing?" she asked, sounding like Mom again. "And Doug, I've put an extra heavy layer on you seeing as you run point in the search."

Doug nodded and squared his shoulder. "I'm ready."

"Count me in," from my partner and his feathered ally.

I boxed us up for the trip. Putting the four of us in a bunch was getting to be old hat for me. In a second, the penetrating cold of Between grabbed us. Too bad I couldn't keep some of that around when we hit the crater again. After half a minute, my internal GPS said we'd reached the rim. I popped out for a nanosecond to take a visual and verify our exact location. I made the necessary correction for Doug's effective cross grid inspection.

Obscuring film or not, fire suit protection or not, this methodical back and forth was as close to Hades as I cared to get. The plumes of steam did their thing, while arrows of flame jumped erratically up from the base of the crater. Back and forth, back and forth, stink and sizzle. Sizzle and stink. Nothing about our present activity came close to making me feel like a hero. Pack mule was more like it.

"I think I see something," Doug whispered, pointing. "Can you nudge me in a little closer—over there?"

What an idiot. Did he forget who'd flipped him from one side of the island to another? Did he think I couldn't do close quarter maneuvers?

"Sure," I whispered back. "I'm here to serve."

Hillary shot me a dirty look. Jakup wasn't so subtle. "Stifle it, Partner. You signed on for this. Do your job."

The area he'd pointed to was on the rim wall opposite where we'd started our survey. What attracted his attention eluded me. Maybe those deep brown streaks. I began an approach and flared about twenty meters from the wall.

"This work?" I asked.

"Umm, yeah."

"All of us or do you want to fly solo?"

Jakup answered for him. "We'll ride along. The obscuring layer tends to stay thicker when we're all together."

As if someone or something heard him, as soon as his words were out, a blue and gold fireball headed in our general direction. Followed by a potful of more than random fireworks-like display. None came close—so far—which proved they hadn't spotted us, but apparently our opponents modified the braille method and shooting off missals randomly in the direction of where our voices originated..

"*Let's hope they don't get in a lucky shot,*" I had to mindsend on a tight circuit so we'd not be overheard. "*We better stick to non-vocal from now on.*"

"*Ten four, Partner.*"

"*Can you hear me now?*"

"*Of course.*" That had to be Kiki.

"*Mostly. Can you project more?*" Doug naturally.

I didn't pick up response from Hillary so I tuned into her mind. She "felt" the intrusion and thought, "*I can't seem to get the hang of this mindsend thing. I guess I need more practice.*"

"*Okay, until you do, I'll check in like this.*"

"*I don't much like anyone inside my head, but under the circumstances ....I'll keep trying.*
"

I moved us up and toward the wall in the zigzag routine I'd seen once in a war movie. Another lucky maneuver. A barrage of fireballs exploded right under us. I wondered how much firepower they had anyway.

Up, over, left, right, down and back up. I kept the bob and turns erratic so the bad guys wouldn't pick up any pattern. Their response suggested they focused on the vocals, but I decided to play it safe anyway. The constant shifting called for more concentration, and I was sweating worse than after I ran a 440. I wouldn't last at this rate.

"*I spotted something— over there by—the triangle shaped slash,*" sent Doug.

"*Something in the crevice for sure,*" I mindsent Jakup. "*Hover near the entrance so Doug can reach in.*"

I moved in and made like a helicopter about a foot and a half from the entrance. Doug breathed deep and extended his hand in slow motion. I understood his hesitancy.

This meant a lot to him, love and life, no less. He wiggled his fingers and stuck his arm into the crevice elbow deep. He came out twice as fast with his arm covered with orange wormlike things. Half-animal, half-bizarre flower. They must have had spines, maybe venom. I could feel his pain.

"We're outta here."

I backed us out and headed for the opposite wall where we'd started our mobile sauna.

A swing and a miss.

CHAPTER FIFTY

Then all hell broke loose. They'd duped us. The voices I thought were some of the thrill-seeking tourists on the rim tour to ooh and aah over the lava flow weren't. I could pick out some voices I recognized.

"Lief, you man the catapult. We gotta bring the interlopers to ground."

"Righto, mate."

The first was our old friend the snake waiter and the second I had no problem recognizing as Lief, Hillary's no-class ex. I couldn't help thinking the odds she'd take him back just went down faster than the next Cleveland Indians winning the next series.

"I think the bad guys pulled a fast one. They deliberately missed to drive us over here."

"I concur," from Doug.

"Trust a human to use bad judgement. Thanks a lot for endangering our lives," Kiki added.

"Chill, Partner. They may have played right into our hands."

Hillary said nothing. I guess I was right. Lief had just cooked his goose with her.

"How?" I asked.

"You pop us in and out of Between. No more than, say, five seconds each time. Relocate in Between and repeat."

"And does that solve our problem? They have more fire power than we do."

"So we lob as many as we can back in their direction. I'll grab the missiles and flip them Between. On the rim, on the other rim, wherever they show themselves."

"Great idea," I said as I went Between and took us some fifty meters catty-corner from where we'd stopped.

"Wait, wait, wait," finally some input from Hillary. *"We need to make sure there aren't any tourists mixed in among them. Not only is this the right thing to do, keeping them safe reinforces our pure at heart status intact."*

"Good call, Hillary," said Doug.

"About time one of you humans uses that big brain you're rumored to possess," Kiki snarked.

"She's quite right, Partner. Using innocent persons as shields is standard field operations for the war gods,"

"Gotcha," I answered, and, in one of our brief pauses in our own world, I hovered over the rim and spotted a half dozen early risers. I sent a strong suggestion to the big

one with the Budweiser belly to pack up and get on to the next viewing spot. He rounded up his fellows and off they went.

I resumed the zigzag up-down maneuvers I'd used earlier. Jakup and Kiki served as spotters for the fireballs and screeches the gods were lobbing in our direction. Piece of cake to nudge 'em back in a parabola toward their point of origin. The screams and curses that ensued were music to our ears. I did some major hair-splitting and didn't aim at them directly. Pure of heart, after all. If some accidentally landed on a living being, not my problem.

"You do realize we can't kill them, don't you. Gods are immortal after all. Lief and some of his ilk might be vulnerable, but the others will live to wreak havoc another day," Doug, the rational scientist among us, remarked.

"Duh," I answered and continued to execute my usual and excellent evasive maneuvering.

"And I suspect even hurting them enough to make a difference might cancel our good guy credentials."

Great. I'll stick with the accidentally defense.

From the sound of things on the rim, our opponents were not happy campers, but the shaking of fists and blind firing of missiles wasn't going to deter us. I picked up the zigzag where I'd last zagged before Doug went in the crevice and pulled out some ghastly creatures that must have come straight from hell. His arm was red and swollen, and I didn't like the pained expression he was wearing.

"Your arm and hand working well enough to pick up the Mark?"

"Barring an ark-sized thing, yeah. I've got to get myself together if I want to marry Darcy."

My partner and I shared a mental smirk at his inadvertent funny. Right Doug.

Between coordinating the sideways movements with vertical ones and dodging fireballs, I didn't pay attention to much else around us.

"Bogey at ten o'clock," Jakup sent on a tight band.

"Yeah, I know, I've been avoiding those all along."

"Human! Gotta love 'em," Kiki chipped in. *"You got eyes? Listen to your partner."*

I took a sideways glace to one o'clock and spotted what appeared to be the world's most ugly woman – boobs hanging off to one side, snakes for hair, claws on her hands—hanging in mid-air pulling fire bombs out of a wickerish basket.

"Hoo boy, now we got trouble in spades. Doug, you better locate the Mark toot sweet or we may end up on the wrong end of a wiener stick over this bonfire."

"Bogie below us, better take us up, Partner."

For the first time in my life, I felt some sympathy for the flies and gnats immolating themselves on the insect sizzler. My life was flashing before me and even the anatomy lab seemed preferable to where we were at present. How long our obscuring fog would last was one question. How long our fire suits would continue to be effective was another. I'd even agree to a year of picking up dog poop to get out of here intact.

"*Wait, wait. Over there,*" Doug sent, pointing, his excitement penetrating every word. "*See the light?*"

Not really, I thought.

"*Let's hope we don't have another dud,*" I answered as I changed our incline slightly to head over to the spot he indicated. I dangled Doug over the area, making him a greater sitting duck than he'd been. We must have resembled a boatful of guys fishing for piranhas.

He reached out and grasped at the object only he had seen. The glow seemed to rise to meet him. I was impressed. The thing he was aiming at was about three foot high, but didn't have much depth. The dent in the made the tablet resemble the pages of an open book. Sort of like two notebooks side by side. The second his finger touched the edge, his entire body appeared to emerge from the steam vapors whole and completely visible. He grabbed the two sides of the table, panting with the effort. The Mark must've weighed a ton. He turned and twisted to rejoin the group clamping the tablet between his body and ours.

An incredible sense of peace filled us and contentment surrounded us. If we all looked as awestruck as Hillary, we made a silly looking bunch, like a bunch of three-year-olds meeting Mickey Mouse for the first time. The same expression kids had waiting in line for Santa Claus.

"We did it," I shouted. "World peace."

I must have shouted this aloud because in the next ten second a dozen fireballs hit us and bounced off. Figures rose around us, and I heard Lief yelling, "Got ya, you suckers."

CHAPTER FIFTY-ONE

Obscured or not, the gods had our number. In their eagerness to lay hold of the Mark, dozens of figures, garish and misshapen for the most part, arose to wage a siege on our small bundle. I recognized the fat form of Kū-ka-ili-moku, the Hawaiian hot shot, trailing a female dressed in a sari, Durga—I think. Most acted as if they were at a loss as to where and how to attack and were shipping random fireballs off in our general area. One, however, a kind of good-looking dude with abs I'd kill to have, moved in a methodical way to narrow the area where they thought we might be.

"Pitiful humans, you have stolen my tablet once, you'll not rob me again," he shouted each time he launched another missile.

"*Mars, that has to be Mars. Our family story said we made a bargain with him,*" said Doug.

"*Uh huh,*" I said, thinking thanks a hell of a lot professor. How's that supposed to help us out of this mess.

Mars must have sensed us somehow. His next volley hit us square on. Our envelope provided some protection against a glancing blow, but with the direct hit, our little group split, spilling us out. Jakup and I went up, Hillary and Kiki stayed put, and Doug, weighed down by the table, was falling straight down into the depth of the caldera. Mars and the sneaky snake god were pulling on one side of the tablet, Doug holding on in a death grip to keep the Mark.

Unless I did something toot sweet, his death grip would be literally true. I executed a flanking movement, picked up Hillary and the obnoxious owl in the process, and dove down toward Doug. I unfurled a psychic rope to him, but with both his arm looped around the Mark, he couldn't catch the line, far less hold on. With Doug less hidden in the diluted shell of our envelope and more visible, he was an easy to spot target. Mars charged and hit him with a tackle worthy of a NFL lineman---or a women's soccer forward. Laid out, tipped back, Doug was an easy victim for the god to grab the Mark.

Doug shot us a hopeless glance, then let the tablet go rather than allow Mars to capture the stone slab. Straight as a die, the Mark careened down and down with Mars and his companions chasing after. Some were so intent on capturing Doug and the tablet, they didn't see the glistening hand of Pele emerge from the lava to grasp the Mark. Too intent, they didn't watch where they were going and hit bottom. They might not die, but they'd be damn uncomfortable for a long time.

All at once, the same thought occurred to us. We felt---we alone---were responsible for future wars and violence. Talk about your bummer. We'd failed in our mission. Doug was solid —and might die solid—but our hopes for world peace were shattered. I bent my head and barreled down. At least I could salvage his wedding plans.

Sometimes fate steps in to save the day. In this case, Pele. The Mark surged flashed and faded into the heart of the volcano. A sudden cloud of steam and vapors arose, shutting off the tablet from sight. I took advantage of the gods' abandonment of Doug to retrieve him. In the moment he rejoined us, a deep voice echoed through the caldera. "The Mark safe shall stay safe in my purse until humans show they are ready for peace. Their minds and bodies must mature to tolerate peace, and they must no longer play at war to overcome boredom. Rest easy, young pure-hearted adventurers, no god will dare steal the Mark from Pele. Heed well, ye gods of war. Snatching that which the greater gods have left as salvation for humans is not a fair fight. The universe mandates a yin for every yang. If you try to steal the Mark of Camael,you will guarantee your undoing."

I heard the furious tone in the voices below us. I decided the best course of action for me would be to move us the hell out of there and 'ported us back to our hotel.

CHAPTER FIFTY-TWO

The sad circle on the balcony of our suite appeared nothing like the young adventures we'd been when we arrived. I'd buy the pure-hearted—after all, we didn't end up fried. I decided some of some of Napa's finest was the best way to drown our sorrow and chagrin with our failure and 'ported some in to a grateful group...

"Bottom line, guys, we choked and failed miserably."

Kiki surprised me saying, "At least you tried, and, for humans, you came close."

"Came close only counts in horseshoes and hand grenades," Hillary said.

Speaking in clichés was so out of character for her, she must be mega-upset—not that the rest of us weren't. I opened my mouth and started to engage my vocal cords, but Doug's monotone interrupted me in mid-inhale.

"Pele will keep the Mark safe. We've still got a chance war will end."

"Yeah, when," my partner asked. "Not any time soon is my bet. Face the facts, even with Kiki's and my help, this mission was a failure."

At least he admitted the feather contingent wasn't perfect—a definite step up in our relationship, Once again in mid-inhale, Doug spoke up. "You must not have heard all Pele said. She appeared to consider our efforts worthy. As I acted as head-seeker, the one with the primary responsibility of recognizing the Mark in the midst of all the fire and foul vapors, she shared a bit of her plan for the Mark. What she said was, "When the peoples of the earth strive to achieve pure hearts and make a genuine effort to end their conflict, I shall return the Mark into the light, once again stand on the summit of the highest mountain, and peace shall reign."

"Wow."

"This means we started a process to peace and others must take on the task," Hillary said. "I hope our leaders..."

Kiki and Jakup stopped their wings in mid-high-five, and I voiced the end of her sentence. "have the balls to do it."

"Not quite the way I intended to phrase my sentence, Riley. We've been so divided and prospects for warring to end don't strike me as good any time soon."

We all took another gulp from our glass, Jakup and Kiki included. So near, yet so far. We'd snatched failure from the jaws of success. With Every eye in the room focused on the floor when Jakup hopped up on the rail and announced, "C'mon guys, J&R did it again. If Lief's not convinced to leave Hillary alone, I'll give up peanuts. Look at

Doug—standup man, you're solid, plainly visible. We'll be hearing wedding bells soon."

"You're right," Hillary and I said in unison. Hillary added. "We might not have achieved the bigger goal, but we're good matchmakers."

EPILOGUE

The last note sounded and the final piece of wedding cake was history, Doug and Darcy on their way to their honeymoon at the Sandia Lab. Not my idea of a good time, but to each his own.

Hillary and I perched on stools at the bar while Jakup teetered on an empty beer mug.

"No complaints on the food," Jakup remarked. "Plenty of peanuts, bits of fruit, berries. Kind of lacking in protein, but I can visit the kitchen for that."

His idea of protein and mine didn't match, so I turned to face Hillary, "She wasn't what I expected, Darcy, I mean. I thought if she was set on Doug, she'd be a nerdette. Instead, she's good looking, with a wicked sense of humor, and outgoing—proves opposites attract. Gotta admit I've never spent this much time in one place with this many tech-weenies."

Hillary ignored my dork-dissing and said, "I liked her. She'll be good for Doug. Make him more outgoing—and talk about brainpower. We'll be reading about them one day."

"You think so? Something you saw?"

"More like sensed. The two complement one another. The strengths of one compensates for the weaknesses of the other. Nothing bad—all positive, I believe."

"Good to hear," Jakup said. "They'll probably win one of those Nobel prizes for a scientific breakthrough. So how about our future? I picked up a message from OWIS about a juicy case waiting for J&R's special skills. . Ya ready to jump back in?"

I stared into space for what seemed forever, but I finally got up the nerve. Almost afraid of what her answer might be, I asked, "Wadya you say, Hil? You want in? If you add your farseeing ability on top of my psychic talents seasoned-well with Jakup's...uh, special skills, we'd have the recipe for an unbeatable team. How 'bout we make J&R a trio?"

"I might consider it," she said.

We chugged the mugs and left together—and she let me hold her hand.

"We'll have to do something about that name though," she mused as we left.

Dedication and Acknowlegement

Without the help and support of my friends, family, and particularly members of critique group and beta readers, this book would never have seen the light of day.

Thank you from me, from Riley, from Jakup, from all the weird creatures born from a weird imagination.

♦ ♦ ♦

www.ingramcontent.com/pod-product-compliance
Lightning Source LLC
Chambersburg PA
CBHW031337060726
47590CB00007B/2512